33 Crystal Skulls
& The Anti+Christ

33 Crystal Skulls & The Anti+Christ
UNCENSORED, UNEDITED, RETRACTED INVENTION VERSION

1ST EDITION MANUSCRIPT. BOOK 5 OF 7

E-BOOK   978-1-967897-05-6
PAPERBACK   978-1-967897-15-5
HARDCOVER

**33 Crystal Skulls & The Anti+Christ
Chapter 11 & 12, PART 5 OF 7**

Dedicated to

GOD

In God we trust.
Our true spark of, cosmic static, spiral core of all our inner sparks, ghosts / spirits. Whatever the force within us, is called.

God is perpetually awesome.
Thank you God for everything.
Please forgive our iniquities. 1971-2666
All material is copyrighted, and may not be reproduced in anyway, without written

HE SEES THROUGH YOUR EYES, HE FEELS
YOUR VIBRATION OF MOVEMENTS, AND INDUCES ALL
YOUR THOUGHTS FROM THE BEGINNING. BUT GIVES
YOU CHOICE. OMNIPOTENT. THE EYE OF RA. SEE
YOU LATER. Y=O..O=S

THANK YOU GOD FOR EVERYTHING.

IN GOD WE TRUST. GOD IS WITHIN. GENOME.

The Human breath of life. An internal, Autonomous program, for humans, extra sensory boost of pure life. An

BOOK 5 CHAPTER 11 & 12 PART 5 OF 7
978-1-967897-15-5

CHAPTER ELEVEN

The Electronic Age of The Demon's, **Y=O..O='S!**

**The Electronic Age of The
Demon Y=O..O='S.**

As, another soul goes in the Gate of
Realms by the name of Jobe. Jobe knows where
he is at, the Gate of Realms, and says.

"Blessed is our God, and thank you for bringing me here, to my Creators home. I ask only two question, your greatness. Why were some humans the way they were? And what happened to the 13 Guardian and fallen Angels?"

Saint Peter, says.

"Jobe, you are a good man, with all the evil that occurred to you were tests, by God. God rewarded you, by giving you more then you ever had before, or would have had if he did not put you through your trials. Now, welcome home my son, and watch."

The story goes that in heaven God made all the Angels, and God was bored with everyone needing nothing ever. All was peaceful in heaven, and then God decided to

select a few Angels to have the power of
choice, and God would monitor, for
entertainment the select Angels he chose.

Well, from the first, Elite Angels
there was, Lucifer, Michael, Gabriel,
Raphael, Chamuel, Zadkiel, Cassiel, Saran,
Satan, Cannibel, Dolores, Tommy and
Dragkkkon. All humans, and souls were all
created at once, and all that would exist,
was created. God glimpsed the future, of
mankind, and decided to create a grapevine
of embryos miles, and miles long for storage
of the souls that would contain the souls
that were not bad or good. But in a comatose
sleep till God decided what to do for
judgment day.

The grapevines were for the
borderline souls that God used for storing

souls, until they were given a second chance for reincarnation or a test, before Gods rules, and Judges decide their fate. Some were destined to the tortures from The Lake of Fires, for all the bad sins.

The souls trapped in the grapevine for reincarnation would have a worse life then their own original life, as a greater test for the life sentence. If the soul died again without good deeds, becoming an atheist or by suicide, they would have a worse, life sentence, trials, then the previous life before.

God gave us the will, and chance to become better by his rules. So do not wonder why your life sucks or becomes worse. Your attitude, and your choices in life are steered to become your destiny.

If you summon the evil or Holy Spirit, it is by your choice, magnifying your actions causing your outcomes. It is like an automobile, if you take care of it, then it will take care of you to, and take you to many destinies. But if you do not maintain your aura, in a positive way then it will break down, and be a piece of junk that you made it into.

Just like a baby. If you nourish the child, and feed positive mental attributes. Then it will attract positive healthy magnifications. But if you do not nourish, and instead feed it negative thoughts or inductions. Then your child will feel like dying, and have a negative life.

Well, what if that child is you? And you have the chance to make it, a well oiled, machine, or sludge up, non performing wreck. Power of induction is amazing, and that which you mimic, copy, dwells, and absorb, you will become. That is why when you see a group of men or women they are mostly similar since they are around each other a lot. But when you are by yourself, you have the ability to become whatever your thoughts are imposing into you. So beware of the thoughts you induce yourself with since we all have the power of choice, until something abruptly changes your destiny by accident or your actions.

The Angels in the beginning had many choices, and some followed God's teachings, and so he rewarded them with gifts of knowledge, power or abilities. Some of the

fallen Angels in the beginning also,
followed God's teachings to perfection.

Lucifer was the first Angel to
receive the power of choice. Lucifer was
obedient so he was rewarded with lots of
knowledge.

One day God, and Lucifer made an
agreement that God being kind allowed
Lucifer to play games, and challenge other
Angels to see if they truly loved God or
were brainless puppets. All the souls that
were created were to entertain God by
allowing Lucifer to take hold of the power
of influence, and put, to test, the souls.
Lucifer was being allowed a 10th power of
the Holy Spirit. Attempting, to utilize the
power of influencing, on the souls. To try

to make the souls in reality, failed souls, to become, his slaves for eternity.

That day when the Devil went to God, and asked God to be able to take from Jobe all that he possessed to see if Jobe could be influenced, to betray God. But, the Devil failed. God did not interfere. God allowed the Devil to do his mayhem, to take all of Jobe's, worldly possessions, to make him try to curse God. The Devil wanted to take one of the most dedicated from God. (Jobe). He failed, since Jobe had studied the ways of God, and was influenced by the right people as a child.

The Devil would prefer the souls to be ignorant in his ways, and believe that if God does not exist, then the Devils do not exist either. If the Devils make people believe that there is no God then the souls become saddened atheists. This in turns makes the human, think, there is, no Devil. Their evil mission is to take all the souls that were created, and take over heaven. The Devil's mission will cause pain, and misery to souls for eternity with the power that God has given him. But after time God made an equal 13 good, and 13 bad Angels over time.

All the 13 Guardian Angels, still to this day protect, and attempt to guide the souls to the right path.

As for the 13 fallen Angels, still to this day haunt, the souls of humanity, to tempt them, to become like them, and join the evil forces of the Damned. Developing a slime, to induce, the evil, by air borne pathogens. Once human thoughts are wrong, then the Y=O..O='S. Vibrate, the evil to manifest in ones life. Secretly vibrating and waiting for evil doers, to attach and become. To this day, the test of humanity continues, with right, and wrong decisions. Be faithful in your daily lives, as you will cross the line to temptation, and glorious outcomes. God has, put the test into existence, and, are now waiting, for your trials, to expire. Life continues. The Y=O..O='S, will be coming to your city in the near future. Their songs are out, to entice you to their products. Beware.

The Devil has a chance to take the souls that have negative auras, and make Hell on the planet for them. Your thoughts, and actions make the opposite, as it was written in the good book. This planet allows you to mentally be in heaven on the planet being optimistic, and focusing good thoughts, and magnifying your aura to bring forth that which is good. But if you are pessimistic, then you will bring the negative Y=O..O='S, to you. Beware. All of us have experienced these natural occurrences, these phenomena that bring forth this chance of good or bad occurrences. Beware.

Jobe enters the Gate to where the 13 good Guardian Angels dwell, to live with.

Back at, The Gate of Realms.

A man by the name of Paul, is released from The Grapevine Cells, and appears in the court yard, and tells Saint Peter.

"I know where I am at. I already know where I am going, so no surprise there. But I want to know, and am allowed by the covenants of all the stories I read, and heard. This is heaven, I know I made it here, and I am a true Catholic, Christian, Jehovah follower, and I know I get two questions. So, my question is. Why did God do all this to us? I read many testimonies of all religions. But what was the real testimony of how it all began?"

Saint Peter says.

"Well, the fact, you asked that question will not change the fact that you will be going to a warm place for quite sometime. There will be no lawyers to help you as most councils, down there, will be getting, the same royal treatment as you. But very well, wise man, close your eyes, watch, and learn. Before your sentence is bestowed upon you. Focus.

There are different heavens, realms, and planets that God actually made. Some more advanced, and some more primitive worlds. Paradises, and worlds with all the souls as happy, and as prosperous as all Angels should be.

As time progressed, God decided to make man kind have their own will, and he started with a select few Angels that stood out from the other Angels. Of course the Devil was one of the first to get this power of choice. The Devils, Lucifer, Satan,

Saran, Charleston, and other evil fallen Angels were chosen but in time were going to follow the Devils. The Pappi Devil was the 13th Angel chosen from billions of Angels.

33 other Angels, had also, been chosen with their own will power, and started using their own minds, and feelings of what was right, and wrong. God saw this was good, and allowed this to occur as, he was entertained by their methods, since life was easy, and everyone was Gods, children. Angels had everything, a soul could ever need or want. So God was entertained by the spirited Angels. The Devilish Angels started to see how God was sovereign over all, and had different, powers beyond any of the other Angels, and saw how God knew all, and could see all.

Lucifer, and Satan, were
experimenting, there own free will. That day
they asked God if Saran, and his Angels
could be masked from Gods ever lasting
blanket connection, and for God not to know
where they were located at any time. Just
like he granted Pappi Devil number leader
one.

God told them if they could convince
more Angels on his Northern side of a
certain Universe in a special Galaxy to turn
against him. Then God would see if their
will or soul could change for someone that
is loved. That would be the challenge, and
God would not know anything, of their Angel
mob if they won, against Gods, truly loyal,
loved Angels. God promised, he would only
glimpse, every now, and then. And assured,
the Angels, just to check on them every now,

and then. And promised them, to not be watching all the time. But light surveillance from time to time.

Lucifer, and Satan were there that day, and teamed up, and not being as smart as God agreed to Gods terms. The Devils traveled the heavens to see what was out there in the new universe. All the Angels which were billions upon, billions in population, began their evolution. They were chosen to be the souls, used for human life. Just waiting for their turns to be human, and alive so we can keep Gods commandments. All our souls in heaven were busy at work happy with a meaning to serve Gods every asking, and never denying God or missing a thing for him.

This is the answer to why people on this Planet say.

"Why does God allow suffering?"

Well. Your soul had it all. Joy, peace, love, meaning of acceptance, and all that if you pass the tests, will once more have. The Devils Lucifer, Saran, and Satan saw the Angels were happy, harmonious, and had it too easy. They pulled pranks, and mischief acts upon any Angels that were near them, making it difficult for the Angels in heaven.

So Satan, Saran, and Lucifer enjoying themselves with there free will, laughed about all their mischief they were pronouncing on the Angels. The Angels would keep going since their minds were innocent,

and without choice. They would keep doing
their daily tasks without any complain.

God loved all the Angels, from
birth. Since, you were always, Gods, perfect
little Angels.

Then Michael seeing all the mischief
that Satan, and Lucifer were doing went, and
told God. God promised the Angels, whom he
would not interfere with them. But asked for
their presence. So the Devils came forth,
and God asked what have you been up to.
Satan, and Lucifer said they traveled all
the heavens, and observed all the Angels.

God said.

"I love my Angels, and they serve me
well, and they are given all they ever
need."

Satan, wanting Gods powers, Satan
said.

"The Angels were dummies, and had no
real feelings of what it would be like to be
worthy of Gods love. That God loved them,
and they did not deserve Gods love like
Satan, and Lucifer should have. Lucifer told
him, that he, should give, Satan, more
powers, to be equal. Like God."

God being loving, allowed him to
have more powers. Satan, and Lucifer were
joined with the other, falling Angels.
Lucifer was showing off the powers Lucifer,
and Satan possessed. They told the other

Angels to join them, and they would not be destroyed, but allowed, to rule, over the other Angels, next to him. He joined forces with 300 Angels that agreed to join him, as these Angels were promised powers like him when they won over throwing God. So, later on Satan went back with his Angel team, to try to over throw God. God promised Satan that he would mask his knowing of what Satan was doing. However, God already knew Satan's plan since Satan told the other fallen Angels the plan.

God was made known as soon as it was recorded in the other Angels minds. God being intrigued that one Angel could influence many other Angels, and allowed Satan to do his little drama. Just to see, what he, was going, to do, next.

Since, God promised Satan he would
not know all with him, allowed him to do as
he was. God having all, knowing all, was
entertained by this little man.

Satan first told God.

" Look. Ira."

And Satan, became a snake. Then
turned into a ram, then a cockroach, and
kept turning into different animals, and
creatures getting closer to God. Then
finally Satan turned into a dragon, and
tried to attack God, while the other Angels
attacked the other 13 good Angels, that were
with God. God not knowing Satan's actions,
looked up at him, and was about to destroy
Satan with a blink of an eye, but just
before he did, his loyal Angel Michael, and

Raphael grabbed him. Tackled him to the ground, and about to cut Satan's head off. All of a sudden all the Angels became frozen.

God froze all so no one would get hurt by each other. Then God chained up all the fallen Angels in gold chains. This would keep the Angels bodies frozen forever. The Angel bodies were frozen but not their heads, and that allowed Satan to talk. God being curious asked why Satan did this.

Satan said.

"That God was foolish to give all the Angels everything they wanted. That the other Angels did not love God as much as our team of Angels did. That the other Angels were just mindless creatures, that did not deserve Gods love. Satan pleaded, with God, requesting, if he had his own planet, he would test these Angels, to see if they were worthy of Gods love."

Satan explained that if they had free will, it would be determined to see if they would adhere with Gods policies. So God being entertained by Satan, and God never having seen an Angel challenge him before, amused him. God was intrigued by this little Angelic snake.

God knew The Devils would lose against God, but being intrigued, agreed. But instead of bothering himself of a battle. God bored easily with a no challenge competition, and said.

"To battle me you must go against souls. An image, but false of flesh with will power of choice, and allowed to learn as all my other Angels have so well. If you corrupt what will be manhood from me, they will side with you to make malicious armies, and ants to fight against me. To be worthy of you, to fight against me. I spared your existence this once, but mock my words, I will not be so generous on the second battle. You will have a leasehold on this Planet. Test mankind and, my disciples will follow my word. Obedient, compliant Angels they are now. I will transfer, one and then two, to this planet for you to, test the loving Angels, full of love. If they come back to me, then they can roam my rooms, for eternity, with their free will. Side with you and they will be yours, for your pleasing. We will have them Judged, by

choosing, few, elite, honest Judges. They
will decide where their life has lead them
to, their chosen doors to open and dwell.
The humans, will be allowed two and only two
questions, to the Judge. If the humans know,
and, prepare, what two questions, they have,
for the Judge. Then let the wise, be wise
with their words, as this is the words for
your question of life. His word will be
final, in his realm.

Go, my children. It is so."

God chooses to not read his mind to
make it a fair battle eons ago. But God
looked into his soul, before he agreed to
make his covenant with him. And saw the
Devil was destroyed, in the end. But it
upset him, to see, that the Devil recruited
many souls.

The only thing is, are you the fallen Angel that strayed a bit but reread manuscripts, testimonies, that lead you back to the written Testimonies of God?

God agreed to the terms, and told the loving Angels to watch over Satan, and his fallen ones, so no other Angel, gets hurt.

God devised a new universe. God created the explosions of rocks, which blew the dust elements, of what we call our universe. So God went out, and blew on dust from heaven that still is traveling around the Universe creating planets, and our playgrounds. So God then created the heavens, planets, the light, the stars, the Sun, and all wonders of the Universe. He

made more layers of heaven of different
worthy levels for the chosen.

Many of his rooms were waiting
rooms, where some but not all Angels will go
to harvest his heaven. That the billions of
worker bees of Angels that watch over the
souls, and future of Angels. On the seventh
day, God rested. The eighth day he went back
to Gods throne room, where the Angels were
waiting.

God says.

"Now Satan, speak."

So Satan, being jealous of God,
Satan again, trying to persuade God, said.

"Let me have a realm, with worlds, where I may test your Angels. To see if they are worthy to be with you, and to see if they are worth your love. If they fail on this planet, let me keep their souls, and do as I please with them, and keep them in my own realm.

This way you will see, all these pathetic souls, these Angels, that are fake, for your true generous, love. Let us see if it is genuine, or not."

God allowed him to be a lease holder, of many Galaxies, and will hold title to the planet for 1,000,000,000 years. God threw Lucifer, Satan, Saran, and the other fallen Angels that joined them to this planet, we are on.

God said.

"I will summon you, Satan, when I want your results. To see what the outcome will be, and those that I send will have their own choices, to do as they please. I will be with them, and not influence them in any way. But put guidelines as I see fit to the situations, to see if they follow or fail."

The Devils were so excited, with their plan, and thought they were going too win.

So God made man, humans with genitals. God first made Adam, a simple man not knowing anything that had occurred in Gods, realm. This was the first Angel's soul, converted to be the first human, to walk on this Planet. God blew into Adams nostrils, and made the Holy Spirit inspire Adams lungs, and he was alive. Adam was happy, and was in the most beautiful part of the Planets tropical island realm called the Garden of Edem. God had the first test created, and they would allow the Devil to use his power to create the Hell some know. God said.

"You may eat any of the fruits but from one tree. The tree is in the middle of the garden, and is the tree of knowledge, the tree of good, and evil. So do not eat from that tree."

God then created all creatures, and allowed Adam to name them, but God knew that they were not a right companion, for him. So while Adam slept, God took a rib from Adam to create the second, transformed Angel into Eve. To be of Adams flesh, and created the first woman, Eve. Adam told Eve that God said they may eat any of the fruits from the plants, but from one tree that was in the middle of the garden. The tree of knowledge of good, and evil. So God loving his works allowed them to be since he promised Satan that he would allow him to do his works on the planet, and God promised, not to interfere.

So God went back to his throne, and, messaged, all the Angels the news, that they would be tested. For all volunteers, would be allowed, to be tested, to be favored by God. Giving them free will on this planet. To prove, that God, was loved, by the Angels, souls. Billions signed up on the list knowing that they would be true, and faithful. Having everything, they ever wanted, would be a challenge, to prove, to God, they deserve to be, in heaven, with God. So God said patience, he will have, the Holy Spirit, bring them down, into human form, when their numbers, were up. God gave Angels, free spirit, to follow, or lead, the victory.

God went back to heaven, to prepare the next souls that were going to be tested. Back at the Garden of Edem, Satan came out as a serpent, to influence Eve, about the tree of knowledge. Satan told Eve, that God did not want humans to be as smart as God, and have his powers, so that is why, they were not supposed to eat the fruit. Satan told Eve to just try it, and that nothing bad would happen.

Eve being young, and naive not understanding, being innocent, and having no real guidance in life, and not knowing all that had happened in heaven decided to try it, and took some to her husband. Adam too being innocent, and having no will power was easily influenced, and ate the fruit.

Now when God came back, he said.

"Children come out, why are you hiding?"

Adam said.

"We will come out but let us cover ourselves, since we are naked."

God said.

"Who told you, you were naked?"

God knew what had happened. God asked Adam.

"Did you eat from the forbidden fruit I told you not to eat from?"

Adam, and Eve lied to God, and God knew all their thoughts, got mad, and threw them out of the Garden of Edem. The DNA, in the fruit, then cursed them to start life as we know it. With the, power of choice, and born naked to start life. With help from God, knowing telepathically, praying to his realm as we are still blanketed with his love. And faith will bring us closer to him, and bring his rooms to our access. As God's gifts are allowed for his followers.

As the Devils still lurks to make
you sway, and feel pain, and suffering for
as long as he wills. God is forgiving, and
knows our thoughts, and sees us as his
children. Since, we were once, in heaven,
with him. He has loved us always, but as a
child that misbehaves, parents punish them
by giving them restriction. But, as time
passes loving parents tend to forgive their
children, as God does to those that love him
back. But, to those that worship, fake
images, fake gods, fake idols that will just
enrage, the true God of ours. Still God
promised Satan, he would not know, what he
was doing, and, Gods promises our bonds,
that cannot, be broken. Since his word is
sovereign.

So then Adam and Eve had hunger
urges, they felt cold, heat, pain, and

unsure of themselves. As time past, God provided for them. God forgave them partially, and humans are humans as they proceed to succeed, and live life. Surely we are going to see death since they ate from the tree of knowledge. Since the juices from the tree of life, still circulate, in all our veins. But God promises immortality on his side of those who carry the faith. As time passed, soon Eve became pregnant, and had Cain, and Abel. Both children were souls of Angels that were brought down from above. All Angel memories are formatted, re partitioned, with simple, code blocks, for the journey. All Angel memories, are wiped out, not knowing the past of heaven, and trip to the planet. Not knowing, why, we are really here, or there. Memory erased.

Adam taught the children what he knew, and kept passing knowledge. Building the knowledge blocks of what is an existence now. God told the humans that God existed, and to worship him, and give offerings to him, as he provides for all. So he wanted, thoughts of generosity. God, creating all, and not needing anything. But tested them to recognize our true Lord.

Cain was a farmer, and Abel a Shepherd. One day they both went to offer to God. Abel brought some choice parts of newborn animals.

Satan went over to Cain, and told him to take the rotting crop over to God since he was not going to eat it anyway. To save the best crop for himself, since the crop is the cream of the crop. Satan told

him, and it was just going to be burned.
Cain agreed, and took some crop, that was
not first choice, as he thought to save the
best for himself for later. Satan told Cain,
to promise him that he would not tell God of
him talking to him. He agreed.

God was not pleased with what Cain
brought, and approved what Abel had brought
him. Cain was very angry.

God knew, what had happen as he read
Cain, and told him.

" Why be angry? If you do well
trying your best, you will get accepted. But
if you do not try, sin is waiting outside
your door ready to entice, and attack you.
It wants to control you and, you must master
control so it won't become you. Team with

the winning side. But I will allow you to make your choices."

Later on that week Satan appeared outside, again to talk to Cain, and told him.

"If you kill Abel, you will be the only one left, to worship God, and, God will have to approve of your offerings, since there will be no more brothers to compete against."

Cain liked the idea of not having to compete and, agreed. Later Cain went to talk to Abel, and killed him, with a crystal rock, he found on the floor. As soon as Abel's blood shed into the airs atmosphere, it screamed to God, and God confronted Cain.

God asked Cain. "Where is your brother?"

Cain said. "What am I his keeper?"

God cursed Cain, and made him confused, a wanderer, and made all his crops not yield the best anymore. As time went on, the population increased. Satan, and his fallen Angels influenced mankind, over generations. Humans were easily overtaken by his influence, since mankind was leaning on doing what they thought was fit, and did not have guidance from God. Because, of his anger of disrespect and, disobedience. God was silent, and observed for Eons. Satan took a heap and, was having a party on this, planet, every day.

God left the world and, did not interfere with the Devils challenge for many Eons. Many Angels got corrupt and, saw that getting everything off the bat was quickly gratifying, but the humans failed the challenge, for the souls to keep. The Y=O..O='S, were most influential and, crushed worlds upon worlds, making mankind, destroy themselves.

More, Eons passed, and the Devils, were getting finally, disgusted by humanity, as their stench grew annoying to the Devils. Their cruelty to each other, was the only thing, most entertaining, to the Devils. The Devils, just wanted, all to suffer the worst deaths. As Satan was the biggest sadist, alive and, loved his home.

Finally God to, was fed up with human ways, their disrespect, their UN-recognition towards God and, the manner that humans learned bad, quicker then good in many souls.

God was enraged at the human race. The Devils masked horns, hid the truth, of the Devils, persuasion, to cause evil, from humanity. Eventually, the Devils, convinced, God to flood the evil out of humanity. As the Devils, scored several points, taking all the souls at once. As some humans were more than 1,000 years old. God decided to destroy life on the planet by flooding it. Before God flooded the planet, God looked to see if anyone still had goodness in him or her, and found only one man, Noah.

As Noah's seed was going to be to the roots to our branches, to start life all over. Satan was too busy enjoying life torturing humans, on the planet and, God seeing only parts of how Satan easily corrupted the Angels. God condemned The Devils to Hellonian underground. Hellonian would contain all the souls, which were doomed, for betraying, the laws and, were to be locked up with Satan, himself.

Satan was pleased with this but did not quickly realize this to was going to be his prison house. Satan had billions of souls that the Devils were locked up with. The complaining souls would bother the Devils, more then it was worth. Being worshiped by souls that had no choice began to bore the Devils. As the demons were slow on thought, and would not process comprehension, very well. Their slow wittiness, infuriated the Devils, punishing them even more, by tormenting the souls with unbearable pain, until they passed out.

So Noah tried to recruit people to help him, and have their souls saved. But humans were to busy in their world as there never had been rain on the planet before. So believing Noah, was impossible to their logic. As some of the humans in those days, lived more than 1,800 years, and never seeing rain. The laws of physics were different.

Water came from the ground to water plants, not from the sky. But Satan was a second voice, and took the world by storm, and the Devil laughed at Noah with all humanity, laughing with him. The communities just kept, drinking, dancing, raping, adulterating, idolizing, and killing as they pleased.

So Satan's plan was to get all the Angels souls to be on his side, and then to overthrow God, when he was not expecting it.

Then finally it happened, and rain drops, started to fall from the sky, and slowly, and surely filled up the planet, killing everyone but Noah, and his family.

Our Grandfather, Noah lighted the candles, and helped us survive to repopulate the planet as we now, know.

God saw that Satan had a right to these fallen souls but was angry at those fallen Angels and, at Satan. Eventually, the

Devils horns had a bad side effect, by having a snake like appearance on his skin. His new natural appearance is why people are scared of him, and why he is now called the number one, evil Devil, Pappi. And made the fallen souls into evil demons, scary looking, but with a hideous appearance. The demons also, had a reduction to their brain IQ, powers, to be goofy like.

Satan took all the fallen souls that were Angels, and realized they were sores in his eye. Satan was not patient, with them. He started torturing them even more, and, enjoying the pain, he was inflicting, on them, for being Angels, in fallen flesh. But Satan wanting sovereign power, he kept trying to influence, the Noah family, and, failed.

Time passes, and, your current life is the outcome. The Devils' vibrations, sound out and, calling you, to be like them. So the world is why it is, because of the promise. You become your own outcome. Use the knowledge wisely, and access the rooms for your future stay.

Satan failed to influence the Noah family, since their hearts were true to God. God realizing, that Satan was influencing mankind, decided, to give mankind guardian Angels to help the weak willed, to outreach the hope, from the trials. He recruited Guardian Angels to deserving humans. Some humans, having two Angels. The Leader Angels were only assigned to certain humans for progression of mankind. This over the years started to allow some of the Angels to start returning back to the second level heaven, where humans would be judged.

Like the story of Noah, all humans thought he was crazy, since there had never existed rain, in their life time. Noah was considered a crazy man, by all that saw him building his arch. Only eight people survived the flood tragedy. But, all the atheists died and, God let their souls go with the Devil.

The Devil was granted to do whatever he wanted to do, with the souls, that were sent to him, and now has a great army of souls, that became demon slaves in Hell. The Devil would then use the souls, to help him influence the future souls for evil, to make God mad and, vanish their souls to Hell.

The Devil was going to take all the converted good Angels that became humans and, lead them to evil ways, to become his future warriors.

One problem that the Devil had, is that, the souls, that God gave, the Devil, had very low IQ, and the demon's minds were similar to that of a 2-5 year-old child. 99% out of 1,000 Demons had this mind deficiency. The other thousands of demon minds, were similar to that of 6-11 year old minds. The bad side effect of the Y=0..0='S, is that they were true, idiots. They even said, that, they are the Y=0..0='S. That they could put apostrophes in their names, as they own everything they want. Willingly or unwillingly.

The Devil was not happy of this curse that God bestowed on him. God did this so that he would give humans a fair chance of having choice, and give leverage to humans and, allow to truly show God that they deserve to be in his heaven.

The Devil was very frustrated over this and, Hell was becoming a large day care for retarded demons. The Devil would take Eons to organize his Hell before he could strike a large scale attack on the humans, then to battle against God. The Devil hated humans and, Angels more then ever and, promised to punish the retarded demons for eternity.

There have been false prophets marketed by the Devil on media like, radio, Television, emphasizing the coming of the rapture and, destruction of false days that they exclaimed to be arriving here on wrong days.

These false prophets have made some believers loose their homes, life savings, made their followers poorer and, some homeless. Making the followers fools to societies. Falsely marking, the atheist, a pseudo appearance, of being correct and, giving their society, a false hope of no God.

These events, that occurred, in the past, are not, further from the truth. These historical events, facts, of what was publicized and, that had been written, made the prophecies more factual. Since, the false prophets, had to appear. The past prophesies were written, so it was already prophesied, by making the events true of the false prophets. The past testimonies, state, there will be, false prophets and, those that are the false prophets, do not believe their own blasphemy. With that said the chronological order of the time line would not happen.

Every thing happens for a reason, fate and, faith coincide with truths of today. To abolish the true events that are occurring, as sign of the historical events. You hear on the news of tragedies, bar fights, riots, murders, adultery, corrupt greedy thieving government officials and, fights in the prisons, on the news every day.

Not only what you hear on the news is all that has occurred in the world. There

are the stories that are not even worth
mentioning that do not hit the headlines.

There are so many events that are
small enough to not be put on the tonight
shows, but big enough to affect a lot of
communities. Effects like solar flares that
brings, depression, and other negative
effects that change the communities by
induction. Some of these effects hit the
cosmos above, and change the magnetic fields
around the masses around you on the planet.
Thoughts of the mind bring forth the
passions, and desires that are morphed to
reality, causing good, and/or bad. These
methods cause attraction to display the
great magnetic field of the planet.

So God blew dust, there was a big
boom, and that is how life from the other

heavens began. The waves are still exploding
over and, over. Expanding, beginning, and,
then ending, on some planets. The rules are
still the same as well as the promises, that
were issued since the beginning, applies as
Classical Law. The inhabited planets are
waiting for our occupation.

Paul is ejected out of the Gate of
Realms, and into the sun for eternity.

ANGEL TOMMY, AND FRIENDS, WANT TO
INVITE YOU TO SING TOGETHER, ONE LANGUAGE.
VIDEO OF ABC, ON YOUTUBE.COM

As the Grapevines of souls releases
another Soul, to Saint Peter, by the name of

Pierre Scholasky. He is now at the Gate of
Realms.

Pierre says.

"I know where I am at. Your Saint
Nicholas in my Country, and I know I get a
wish like king Solomon had."

Saint Peter says.

"Wrong. You do not get any wishes as
you get two, and only two questions, you may
ask me. Saint Peter. Not Nicholas."

Pierre says.

"I will ask since I am an
archaeologist in my Country. I want to know,
what happened to the aliens bones we found,

that use to live on the planet? I know I
have seen so many of their ships, and I want
to know, how did they get so smart?"

Saint Peter says. Very well.

A vision starts:

A long time ago, man was said to
come from Anfrica about 50 billion years
ago. Recently archaeologists found bones in
Chiena with readings up to 300 billion years
ago. However the story for some atheist,
goes that man will not find out about how we
are created, till we go out of our solar
system, and find a more advanced race, other
then ours.

Well we do not have to get on a
spaceship to go find them because the

travelers are already here, on this planet
looking for some of the same thing human
souls search for.

        Just imagine where we will be in 300
billion years from now. We will be so
advanced, that we will be able to go to
other planets, and observe them.

        However, when our astronauts locate
other inferior civilizations, they must
adhere to protocol. The astronauts will not
want to make contact with inferior races, as
protocol deems it necessary. Our advanced
civilization would not give the primitive
people advanced weapons, so they would not
hurt themselves. An object, that could kill,
may also save. As guns kill for food, saving
starvation, as a gun could kill with
maliciousness.

Some inventions are so advance, and could be used for maliciousness that, could kill many individuals at any spot in the world, just by typing a sentence on a screen with commands for possible total destruction, at any location on the planet.

We posses this, top secret advanced technology, that will be discussed to a certain depth today. Certain designated elite humans can push the blow up buttons on their intellect devices. Even click, from their own bathrooms, from any part of the world. Flushing out human life, and hindering progression in certain areas.

All this can be done from designated nano scope capillaries, and implanted to our

epidermis called the Intellect Cyborg Chips.
The (ICC).

This technology is so powerful, no
adult human may use it, as the chips
programming, literally fried, every adult
human brain that ever attempted to inject
the nanobot technology into the Cortex
medulla oblongata. All adults, and some
children that have tried, have had
fatalities. The crystalline serum is said
too only be accepted by intertwining with
uncorrupted specimens.

Some say Hitler knew of this great
knowledge, from reading the stolen scripts,
stolen from the underground Mayan temples,
and pyramids in what is now called Jermany.
There were space crafts there before Jermans
time. Most humans just thought these giant

facilities were abandoned buildings of rocks and stones. The humans would occupy these buildings, not knowing the real purpose, of the coordinates, the buildings were located in. Humans facilitated, and thought the buildings as small work shelters of some sort, and started building around these great facilities.

Hitler was excited, when he discovered the possibility of special mind control, and being ultimate power by a certain blended elixir with golden accessories, that was enhanced on steroids by the turbo crystal engines.

Hitler wanted to try to change the new world order to his liking. This made Hitler want more power, and this new world would only be an exclusive list of people

for this new planned world he dreamed of.
This new world was for only those, that
followed his reign, and order. Otherwise,
all that opposed were killed.

As with more advance discoveries of
the Polar Tricknowlogy, Hitler wanted all
the powers that the legend told of these
mysterious powers as, he was told as a
little child.

Legend goes that in the right
elevation, and with certain passages read
out loud, and the injected serum inside the
host, would allow and, merge that person,
into the outskirts, presence of God's center
point, on the universes. Hitler knew of the
power, and knew if the merger could be
extracted, it could increase the human
responsiveness, and mind control of others

with a simple look into subjects eyes.
Inserting this advance liquid by what was
translated as, Goldra. This would be the
ultimate euphoria.

Hitler thought, he could attempt to
use the technology too win the war. As
Hitlers defeat was imminent. Hitler was more
stressed out and, desperate for anything. He
had already denounced God, as he shunned him
away and, knew he was not anywhere to
bargain, pray, or negotiate with God.

Hitler became desperate, and without
the scientists testing, the final results on
any human, Hitler with little patience or
hesitation was desperate enough to take the
crystal serum himself.

As Hitler injected the fluids in his neck area, where he believed, by translations from the Golden tablets, to his understanding, is the correct location on the neck. The tablet, may have instructed to inject in certain locations of the body, to get the euphoria experience.

Hitler was more overwhelmed then he imagined by the power of the fluids. Hitler was looking into worm holes in front of him. Hitler's mind is overwhelmed, and goes into shock, from his disbelieving of the objects appearing in front of him. All this visions of people, and mass worlds in front of him was too much for his mind, and then it instantly killed him.

As the room smelled of burned charred brain, now flooding the room of the odor, coming out of his ears, from Hitlers miss calculations, of where he injected the crystal serum.

　　　　When Hitler was found, everyone thought Hitler committed suicide. As that was not Hitlers intention as he fought to the last breath of life, he had in his lungs. However, with a BBQ-ed brain, his life would not exist. That is why his cadaver was missing the brain when his body was found. Hiding this info was, to secure the serums, secrets, merged inside the membranes. The rest of his body was kept on ice for DNA, conservation, as the worlds most hated man, with possible mystery serum in his brain. The body is still yet to be confirmed it is on ice, but to your eyes only.

These, so called, aliens, are no aliens. But a branch, of humanity, with knowledge older than most generations, built right in them. They are, an advanced species, with technology, that will be shared with advanced peaceful humans.

Pierre is allowed to be reincarnated as he was borderline. He did not do enough good deeds or bad deeds to be allowed into The Gates of Heaven. The exclusive, qualified, members only, are allowed, into, the Gates of Heaven.

Roberto, is now at the Gate of Realms.

Roberto says.

"Holy guacamole I know where I am
at. I am finally free from that prison,
jail. I believe in Ala, Jesus, and Buddha, I
am saved, hurray. Your Saint Peter in my
Country, and I know I get to be saved
because of the blood from our lord, yippee."

Saint Peter says.

"Wrong. Your faith disallows you to
the elixir life. You do not get any freedom
of speech up here, you were in prison, with
3 life sentences, for multiple murders. I
do not care for your mumbling words of lies.
If you believe or do not believe. I know you
are bad to the bone. Look at yourself with
all those tattoos of glory kills. You think
a Buda tattoo, of a statue is going to save
you. Your literally, dead wrong. Your
discernment made you, falsely believe, in

your own rules, not by the abidance of the written word. Two, and only two questions are what you are allowed to ask me, and be quick.

You may ask me, your question, and yes, it is Saint Peter."

Roberto is surprised, and is looking scarred but his brain asks from nervousness.

"I saw when I was a kid a giant human man, come down from lightning, and then quickly disappeared. No one believed me, and I want to know, were those memories real? What is the story with that, and will humans ever reach that level?"

Saint Peter says.

"This is tricky but yes you did see, what is called a 711G. Very well, pay attention, as this is futuristic technology from a world, you were not use to."

A vision starts.

Some dictatorships or terrorists, would love to have this ultimate power, and make perfect targets for some Countries to use this technology on. This technology exists today, and will be used by certain 711G military groups, when, and if needed.

The only scenario when this great power is going to be unleashed, and used is when, and if more people will live, by killing the opposing nations. Causing disruptions of course, but ultimate majority, survival may be depending on them.

Only a few elite humans will ever hold this technology. There are an elected few with more precise powers that can do these very tasks of ultimate destruction. A computer, printed, Megatron breed, of a special giant guardian unit group, called the 711G.

As those were the true alien technology, brought from other planets, that were equivalent to humans, but were giants. Their transportation portals were so advance, that they used lightning to beam to, and from their destinations. Some say that, one elite individual of the 711G force, has the key to the Gate of Realms, that I have brought you too.

The Gate of Realms has so many rooms that there is no number recorded high enough on human methods of records to tell how many rooms there are. If you used a computer to try to count all the rooms, the computer would still be counting. Then the R.A.M., on the computer would get full, and the computer would have to keep restarting from locking up each time the computer tried to count how many rooms the infinite great Gate of Realms. Rumor has it one of those doorways goes to God himself, but the key code is impossible for any human to unlock. So what else would you do in 300 billion years?

Humans by then will realize this life effort is a brotherhood of invisible communities working together to bring little children their breakfast, and bread in the

mornings for eternity in the background.
Working together unseen but well
accomplished.

God put us here with chapters in our
lives to bring you forth to judgment day.
Humans will be able to cure ourselves with
our own brain making advanced chemicals
within ourselves. Remove cancer with the
thoughts of an acid to be produced in our
own body by will.

With certain modifications to the
brain, and technology from the central
processor chip in a very small part of the
brain, have shown to make a difference.

Most translators of the Bibles
translated the chips to be inside humans,
and not on their bodies. The reality almost

all humans carry on their body, a cell phone with the chips not in humans, but on them, making the prophecies already true. Of course there is a certain chip or what is really just a flake of skin with code that will save lives like the cell phone does, but will be the biggest upgrade you will ever be able to do. These special gifts will truly enhance man kinds already given gifts.

However, most humans forget how to use our promised powers. You have never lost the powers, you just forgot how to use it. Only difference is the loss of focus.

One power within is hypnosis, or what one Latin scientist called it, (Burar, Reprogramar.)

The translation is that the brain is reprogrammed by your internal vision unit. These units could attempt to erase years of negative exposure from all your life. Then reprogramming of new learning events, by implanting visions over, and over, burning a memory image, giving new skills as if you did the new skill process for years. When in reality you just uploaded it by making an image on a flake of your brain tissue. Watching on certain screens, with certain light colors, for human memory recordings.

We all have an idea on how to be hypnotized, and change our positive attitudes, for the better.

Most of us now some days, even know how or have an idea how to hypnotize others, reading minds, moving organs around, slowing our heart beat, speeding our heart beat, telekinesis, and moving objects with our brains or any other thing you can think of that is phenomenal, has history of existence. These chip flakes will give you ultimate progress. They interact with brain tissue, capillaries, blood cells, and make them into little advanced super human nanobots.

Humans' imaginations are very creative. But gets most of the data from communicating through, writing, listening, seeing. The things that our ancestors possessed, passed it onto certain clans, or learned the induction processes, and saw in the past like reincarnation visions. We believe it to be since our instinct senses it, like De ja Vu.

However, it is our ancestor's images, who saw the history of years. And when the ancients had kids, the ancient ones' protocol was to induce the learning to the new members, and were supposed to pass knowledge to the chosen children through induction.

Very similar to the way kittens, pass the knowledge, that induces the kittens to be trained to use the litter box. The training of what the parent cat knows, passes to the kittens through induction. Induction is amazing, it passes, and grabs, and pushes its powers along to whatever is next to it, like electricity, and wires, through transformers, and remote controls, etc..

Evil that has passed through the years has made many humans lose the gifts that God allowed us to have. In the future we will all see, and have the chance to regain the gifts, since we still have the power of choice. The evil Y=O..O='S, spirit is also manifested, and related to the Holy Spirit, but is consumed by induction of the human hosts thoughts, and will power. The time line, until you go to the Gate of Realms. Which is to be enhanced by choices you make every day, giving you a sentence, for eternity. You magnify your thoughts, and the cosmoses give you the opportunity to become. Then you repeat to become your thought.

God has always given you the choice of good, and evil. God just wants you to choose, and believe, as it is your choice to not believe. As the spirits will visit you many times in your life time, allowing you to be consumed by your own will power, and your future to be written by you. Then uploaded to the Gate of Realms. The ending will always be the same, with the Rapture, and Armageddon to be evolved in its own time.

If the Devils could cause the end tomorrow, they would take the alien armies, and all the souls to go fight God. Then it would only be the end for the evil traders, that more then likely knew of God but, failed to believe in God. That is why atheists are hoping there was no God. Futile mistake, as the good still lives to fly another day in the heaven realm. As you see, the other races on other planets did not have the Devil as the owner of the original

Planet. As with technology advances, and not held back by bureaucratic Demons suppressing mankind for fun.

So that is why you see the more peaceful alien species evolve quicker by team work cracking the genetic, and solar spacial travel codes, together as one planet making more advances then violent planets, blowing themselves back to the caveman time. No technology. So the Devils want all the souls of humans, and aliens, to help him, and seize more advanced technology for the war on God, to try to become a sovereign successor, and take the power of Omni Potency. As his disorganized, and organized takes over of planets around the galaxies have allowed him to get a very large army to conquer more planets, and allow his collective to grow to get ready one day, to

fight God. Powers or no powers will not,
make a difference if you are on the evil
side. The only difference is which side will
you be on, when the trials begin for you?

Roberto is, sent to second Judgment.

Saran Judges, second undetermined
souls, that Saint Peter thought was
borderline. Saran normally, sends the souls
to Hellonian. As that is where Roberto is
now sent. Saran deems Roberto guilty, and
must live in Hellonian forever.

Back at the, Gate of Realms.

As Saint Peter receives another soul
by the name of Ronald, and appears in the
court yard, and sees Saint Peter.

Ronald says.

"I know where I am at. Your Saint
Nicholas in my Country, and I know I get a
wish like king Solomon had."

Saint Peter says.

"Wrong. You do not get any wishes,
as you get two, and only two questions, that
you are allowed to ask me, about your life,
or anything on your mind. You may only ask
me the questions, and only me.

You may now ask me, your question,
and it is Saint Peter, not Nicholas."

As they both clear their throats.

Ronald says.

" Well I want to know why I could
not sleep good, why I was a night owl?

Saint Peter says.

"You have the choice, and you will
be part of the end, no matter what."

A vision starts in his mind, and
images of Jesus, Mommed, Buddha, and many
others are mere images of what God put here
as a passage way for good, and bad, but it
is up to your soul to go to the left or
right path. Things that you learn, like add
2 plus 2 together. Somehow there will always

be an answer to your question, but be careful what you ask for, you just might get it. You will always get an answer one way or the other.

We all come from one area or planet, and are being called to go back, with the little green men or Angels in their flying machines. Their Cherubim on little flying saucers, to get off this planet, or whatever you want to call them.

This technology is not for all but for the peaceful, God-fearing individuals that know right from wrong. The ones, that make it, will find out where we came from, and we will be flying instead of driving on tires. Most of us already know that to be the future, and that the instinct, and hunches you know, and feel are true. Our instinct, clairvoyance, 6-10 senses, is like knowing that our father God exists by Gods induction from his blanket around the universe called the Ion field. This is the element that connects everyone to his channels, uploading, and downloading while you blink and when you are asleep.

This is why, humans will go crazy without sleep. If they do not upload the daily events to the so called cosmic air cloud of Ions. As this gets recorded to the Gate of Realms, the big hard drive in the sky. Though, beware as the Devil masks Gods blanket, with his God given powers, and do not steer to the Devils as he is already in your room if your name is on the Wall of Doom by invitation. As your repetitiveness in your life, had no new information to upload, and download. As that is why there was not much activity for sleep needed. As your body is the reason, you slept. You needed to replenish your body. So sleep, and upload your daily activity, to the Cloud of Realms. All memories go here. But you still need sleep, to achieve a good night rest.

Ronald is thrown to the Nova Star, as fuel for the Galaxy. Ronald was a bad person, and only cared about himself, not mounting to any other gate in the sky.

Back at the, Gate of Realms.

A man by the name of Jimmy, appears in the court yard, and looks at Saint Peter with a surprised look on his face.

Jimmy says.

"I know where I am at, this is a
dream, I am not dead. Your Saint Nicholas in
the old Country, and I know I get three
wishes, like king Solomon had, or something
like that."

Saint Peter says.

"Wrong. You do not get any wishes,
as you get two, and only two questions. You
may address me as, Saint Peter, not
Nicholas."

Jimmy then says. Very well, um, I
have always wondered, and I think I want to
ask is. Were we really lizards or monkeys
from day one, on this planet? As some

scientists have said. Or what was the deal
with that, there?

The visions occur for Jimmy.

There are many archaeologists that
want to know where we first came from. Were
we first created, or did we first crash land
on this planet, with lost technology.

Many stories suggest that what
happened in a distant planet originally came
from our planet journeying for more vacant
planets to posses. We had a few scout ships
monitoring this planet 300 billion years ago
with what would be a futuristic space craft.

There was a malfunction from an
internal blast, and hit a voyaging passenger
shuttle, and damaged other nearby ships,

making the ships go out of control, and

having the ships crash in different parts of

the planet.

       All survivors were lost in one ship

and, the other ship landed in the ocean.

Only a few survived and, washed to shore.

The air, sun and, atmosphere in the year was

different, then the air, they were use to

breathing. The bacteria made these aliens

immune system have a battle, to adjust to

the new living atmosphere, and created this

new race of fewer inferior beings. Compared

to what originally came from their previous

planet.

       As time went on, the elders that

would of passed the induction process to the

younger beings, died, in the crash. The

advanced knowledge, was now lost, forever.

The old, and wise did not give the children, the special powers of learning, of how to find the power within us, or themselves.

Cavemen were born. There were few children that allowed their immune system to adapt to the new atmosphere becoming muscular, and now habitable, and livable. As time went on more of the powers were lost, and illness, and inflammation occurred to these poor beings. It was a new colony that started this race on these other planets, since the famous story of Adam, and Eve. Evolutions from the first seeds have blossomed to other Galaxies. Some current, peaceful planets, holding all the technology as it is now. Hidden on purpose, or by accident. Being floods or fire explosions, bring the planet back to an Amazon planet.

Back to the so-called primitive cavemen period.

        Adam, and Eve did exist on every new planet a different but a similar story. Sometimes groups of communities migrated to new planets. But, it was not on this planet that started their population, but another similar planet not too far away. Not this time around. As histories hard drives, keep recording, in all mass around us. To tell all, at the Gate of Realms.

        Adam, and Eve had their chance but when God got mad at them he cursed them, and humanity, more then once. But yes, that crawling snake of the Devil, did conceive with humans, and some humans hide the lizard you say you ask about.

There are still pages of the
original Bible that have not been found, and
the churches did not put all the testimonies
in the original Bible. The churches did what
the chapters in Revelations told them not to
do, (Add or take away from the original
Bible). God has destroyed the planet you
were on a few times already. No one knows
exactly how many times the big guy has done
it, but it has been done, all over the
universe, too humans in justified planets.

The Devil's armies are getting huge.
This time around the Angels, and the Devil
will battle it out, and take the souls for
eternity, not allowing them to be
reincarnated. As the Devils want your soul
the first life time around, to place you on
hold, in his Lake of Fires. Not everyone
gets reincarnated, as even in the Bible it

says, not to believe to be reincarnated. The
Devils do not want to wait for second life
chances, or even third life chances. It all
depends if you are lucky enough to be
reincarnated, and skip the waiting list. The
Devils want your soul now. As we are the
Aliens to the planets, some just dumber,
and/or smarter, then the rest of other
inhabitants, in the Galaxies.

        Jimmy is sent to the next Realm to
get cleaned of his sin, and is allowed in
the Gates of Heaven.

        Back at the, Gate of Realms, a man
by the name of Daryl, appears in the court

yard, and asks Saint Peter the normal questions.

Daryl says.

"What just happened? Where am I?"

Then immediately a vision starts.

Things in life make some mad, and others go crazy with certain things that occur. A newly 21-year-old Nebrasca guy, by the name of Daryl, is getting ready to go with his friends, and family on an adventure get away for the 4th of July to play, and try too win in Los Vegaz. Daryl is so excited to try to win in Vegaz with his new crisp $1.. A dollar bill, he had earned for watching his baby brother. Daryl just turned 21, a few weeks ago, and has high dreams to

become a millionaire. His friends, and
family are all packing, and getting ready to
go to Vegaz.

Daryl was talking, and bragging how
his Georgie Washingtun was going to make him
rich, and he was going to go places with his
one dollar bill. He goes, and brags to all
his neighbors how he was not coming back
with his dollar. But will become a multi-
millionaire, and be brought back in a limo,
from all his winnings. His limo will pick
him up at the airport, from his private jet.
And all haters, could kiss his butt.

As they arrived to the Hotel in Los
Vegaz, they immediately went to the Buffet.
Daryl finally saw the machines and thought
to himself. That is going to be the machine
that is going to make him a billionaire. The

Spinerator 711 slot machine. It was known
that this machine made more millionaires
than any other machine in Vegaz.

        The line was so long to spin the
wheel, it reminded him of the arcade he use
to play when he was a kid, and had to wait
in line just to play a video game. But not
now, this was different, this was real mans
game, where it would change his future
forever, and he now was legal to drink, and
he could not wait to get comped a fresh cool
drink for free, as he waited in line. He was
ready for the long haul to wait in line,
since he was showered, clean, and he had his
fresh gear on. He wore his baggy pants, that
were almost hanging, to his ankles. His
underwear was sticking out. And his not
washed undies were exposed from his pants,
hanging so low. Daryl was sporting his cool

big shoes, with criss cross shoe laces. He
was wearing an oversize green T-shirt with
the logo Hobo 9 Gang gear, and a bandanna on
his head.

Daryl was ready for the long haul,
to wait in line for his turn. He was trying
to catch a waitress, to get that fresh drink
filled with 80 proof alcohol. Since he
deserved it, since he was a player there at
that casino, he deserved it. As Daryl is
waiting, he hears the sound of. Cha-ching,
cha-ching, bells whistling, screams of joy,
and on the intercom he hears code 389 at
station 33. He looks over, and over, about
500 people in line, waiting for their turn
at the chance to win on the Spinerator 711,
slot machine. The machine only costs a
dollar to play, and the slot machine is a
giant machine. Making sounds, and sounds of

victory for the lucky person who just spun.
The player just spent seven dollars, and he
won $300,000.

        Daryl is thinking, he had just
enjoyed a superb buffet, with Mom, and Pops,
that treated me, and I did not have seconds,
I went, quadrupled style on that buffet. I
grinded on all those delicious plates. MMM.
The meal was really good, and those tatter
tots were mouth watering. And all four times
I went back, it was better each time. Maybe
I went five times with dessert, all I know
is Pops is cool, since he also bought me,
this souvenir drink holder, of the hotel,
and it was still quenching my thirst. But I
am ready for that drink from the waitress.
As he slurps the last drink from the crazy
straw. SSSLLLRRRPP. The cool blended

watermelon Icee was slurpalicious, as Daryl licks his lips, and says.

"Where is she, I know it is busy, but I want my drink, I am a paying patron?"

As Daryl sees the waitress and says.

"Oh there she is Waitress, Waitress. Darn I missed her."

As Daryl then thinks. While I am still waiting with the money in my hand ready to play, and get my big bucks.

As he reached into his pocket he pulled out his lucky pink rabbit foot, and said out loud.

"With this lucky rabbit foot that has kept me going, and has gotten me lucky with all the girls. Will make me rich today."

Even now he felt women, were checking him out. In reality they were seeing him as a big loser since his dirty stinking underwear was out of his pants. As he thought, he knew they all wanted to touch his rabbit foot.

He thought. But I was no sucker, I was not going to give my rabbit foot to just anyone, Daryl thought.

Then coincidentally a short little 21-year-old ex girlfriend that Daryl dated for eight years named Jessica was in the same Hotel for the fourth of July, and says.

"Hey Daryl what are you doing here? Oh you also brought your lucky rabbit foot. A boy that sure does like a nice lucky pink rabbit foot, and that is a nice belt buckle of a horse shoe. I'll bet you're real lucky, with those good luck charms. I'm going to go play a dollar I found in one of those slot machines on the floor, and I was about to go play it on the other side of this casino, since the lines to long for this slot machine. But I don't have any lucky charms like you, so I was wondering if I could hold your lucky pink rabbit foot you're holding. It sure looks lucky."

Daryl rolls his eyes, and thinks to himself.

Heck no, if I let her hold it, and she goes to the other side of the casino, she will just steal it, and I won't be able to get back in line where I am at. It's almost my turn.

Then Jessica says.

"If you let me hold the lucky pink rabbit foot, and if I win. I will give you half of whatever I win, and I'll let you give me a kiss. It shows looks lucky."

Then Daryl lifts up his Hotel cup to his lips, holding melted watermelon ice, and slurps up mostly air, and closes one eye, with a mad dog look in his eye, and says.

"NOOOO."

Remembering why he broke up with her. Since she was so possessive, and she ate the last, Juju Bee, from his box at the last movie, they went to go see, together. Even though, she had to pay for the movie tickets. Then Daryl says.

"Get your own lucky charm. I am not sharing, my luckiness with no one."

Then Jessica starts yelling at him.

"You no good for nothing, BOY. You need to get a job, and stop living with your parents, and do something with your life. I hope to God I win, and do as you said, and not share it with you."

Then she is so mad she wants to leave the Hotel so she can stop looking at him, and gets next to a slot machine, and put her dollar in. Pulls the lever, and all of a sudden her anger turns to tears. Bells start screeching, lights start flashing twirlers start twirling, and spinning. Then she realizes that she hit the jackpot. She won $105,000. Dollars with her coin. Just like that. People gather around her, and take pictures, and congratulate her, and about an hour goes by from all the commotion, she totally forgot about Daryl. Then after all the commotion settles in, and she is walking away from the cashier box, she passes Daryl, still in line, and she sees him. Smiles at him, and says.

"Keep your dead rabbit foot, and I don't need it."

Then Daryl grins sadly, and said.

"Are we still splitting what you won?"

Jessica laughs, and says.

"Rub your pink rabbit foot, and shove it up your butt. Good bye."

Then Daryl looks over the line, and it still is very long, and all that liquids, and buffet starts churning in his stomach, and he is not feeling all that good. Daryl, asks the senior citizens in front of him, and in back of him if they would save his spot.

Both front and back people in line agree and say.

"Hey buddy you leave your spot, you loose your spot. We are not going to baby sit your spot."

Later on that evening Daryl is still waiting in line, and the line is still long, and he is still being positive. Since he knows if Jessica got lucky, he knew he was going to get real lucky. And win his multi trillions of dollars. After hours of waiting in line, and him hearing bells, whistles, cha-chinging, and twirlers, and people winning all night, there were only a few people in front of him. He thinks to himself, only a few more people in front of him, and he knows he can hold going to the bathroom. Daryl keeps trying to catch a waitress but all of them are real busy, and he hears the cocktail waitresses in the casino keep yelling cocktails, cocktails, and then finally he catches a waitress, and says.

"Yea baby, go get me a Rum, and Coke, and a big tip will be given to you after I win the big bucks on the Spinerator 711."

She smiles, and says.

"Sure honey."

After a few more spins, and it's going to be finally his turn. He looks around, and the waitress he orders his drink from is no where to be found. Then finally it is his turn to spin, but he knows if he goes, and uses the dollar, and he doesn't get his drink he won't be playing on the machines, and he won't get his free drink. So he stalls the line, and starts doing the pipi dance since he is almost exploding inside. The people in the back of the line behind him are yelling.

"Come on buddy, move it, play it or leave."

Then finally the waitress comes with his drink, and says.

"Here you go sugar. I hope you won big, for that big tip, you said you were going to give me."

Daryl says.

"I still haven't played. I'm going to play now."

She says.

"Whatever, good luck."

And walks away.

An announcement is heard on the speakers.

A commercial is heard, and the singing begins by saying.

"Mega Megatastic, cola is so yummy, yummy sola, cola yummy yummy cola is caffeine cola, yummy yummy cola, drink it everyday, yummy yummy. Go, and power up, and buy my yummy yummy Mammi for my tummy, yummy

yummy, for my tummy, yummy yummy, Mega, Mega, Mega, Mega, Mega, Mega, Mega, Mega, Yummy, Megatastic colaaaaaaaa."

        Here it was, the moment that Daryl was waiting for. He hears bells, whistles, cha-chinging, and twirls in the background, and he knows it's finally his turn. He starts imagining how he's going to waste his money, and how he is going to go home in his private jet, and ride home in his limo playing the loudest bass anyone has heard, it's going to be so loud that he is going to be floating over the woofers. He is going to be jumping, dancing, and living the life. Most important he is going to go in front of Jessica, and tells her you should have split your Franklins with me. And I would have given you at least a few of my thousands, from my trillions, I won. He was thinking he was the smartest man on his block since he made his fortune off a dollar, and everyone else had to work really hard. As he is sipping his Rum, and Coke, and enjoying it. All of a sudden he hears people yelling in the background.

"Hurry up. It's late. We still want to go see the fireworks outside. Lets go. Come on, move it. Hurry up. I have to go to the bathroom. Play or go."

Everyone is yelling in the background telling him to hurry up. Daryl wakes up from his day dreaming, and he looks at his drink, and he starts to down that puppy, as if it was water. The alcohol rushes to his head, and he is ready to spin. He smiles, and looks across the room, and

sees Jessica. He gives her the finger, and
says.

        "Yea. Now it's my turn."

        With all the commotion, he forgets
all about his bowl movements. Gets closer to
the slot lever to pull his winnings out.
Closes his eyes, grabs his one dollar bill,
that has tape on it, from being ripped in
the past. Inserts it, into the slot machine,
and all of a sudden, he hears a ring, and it
wasn't just any normal ring he has been
hearing all night across the casino but a
distinctive ring, and he knew it, the sound
of him wining his trillions of dollars, he
knew it. Opens his eyes, looks over to where
Jessica is at, and does a dance, moves his
head like an Egyptian dancer. Gives her the
finger on each hand, and starts Moon walking

like an Egyptian dance. Then he hears people yelling at him.

"Come on idiot, your dollar was rejected put it in again."

Then Daryl wiggles his head, and says.

"What da?"

Then he notices his dollar was rejected, since the dollar bill was old, and had tape on it. Then he tries again inserting his dollar in the machine, and the Spinerator 711 rejects his old worn nappy dollar bill. The scanner does not accept his dollar bill. Then he tries again, and again but it just keeps beeping the sound of rejection. So he gets his dollar changed

with one of the employees that walked by,
and changed it for him with a brand new one
dollar bill. Now he is ready too win it big,
and this time nothing was going to stop him.

Daryl was ready to get what was
coming to him, and by now he was squeezing
his butt cheeks, clenching so nothing was
going to be released from his bowels.

As Daryl is ready to insert the
money.

Jessica walks by, and says.

"That was rude, you giving me the
finger. Why would you do that? Just to let
you know, I feel bad, that I ate the last
Juju bean, or whatever, on our last date.
And if you want, if you win we can split
what you win, with my winnings."

Daryl looks at her, and says.

"Witch you know my lucky rabbit foot keeps bringing you back, and my charm is going to make me rich today. Nice try, I ain't given you squat. Get lost witch."

She looks at him with such anger, and walks away slapping him before she leaves.

Daryl's head kicks back, and he looses the clench he has on his buttocks, and a squirt comes out of his butt moistening his exposed underwear that becomes very visible to everyone that is behind him. Daryl said.

"Shoot, I doesn't care, because I have to get this dollar in the Spinerator 711. And I am going to go, and get a new suit that will be worth more then anyone in this room."

People in the background behind him notice the big stain on his underwear, and the smell that started to blow in the crowds direction. From the heavy flow of air from the a/c blasting in the Hotel. The long line crowd starts yelling remarks to him.

"Hey stinky you have to change those boxers for diapers."

As the long line of people all laugh at him. Next he starts inserting his newer dollar in the machine, and the Spinerator 711 finally accepts his dollar bill. Daryl

is so excited, ready to pull the lever, and
as he does he can no longer hold his
liquids, and bowels. Daryl now reaches over
to the lever, and starts pulling it down
with a hard push since the lever was a bit
stuck. As Daryl pulls the sticky lever with
a push, he feels he has no more clench on
his butt muscles sphincter. His clench gave
in. Which was holding all the feces, and
urine from the buffet. Diarrhea starts
coming out like crazy, from eating five
plates of the buffet. Daryl over did it at
the buffet, like most people, and instead of
going to the bathroom like a normal person,
he waited in line too win his riches. Daryl
didn't care, since he was about too win big,
he could feel it, not just all the Pooh,
that went out of him, but he could feel the
winning coming to him. He got a seven, and
then a cherry, and then, some win big, three

times. Daryl jumped up yelling, and
screaming.

"Yeas, this be it."

As he felt the liquid excrement's
squirting, and going down his legs in a
massive stench bulk. But there were no
whistles, no bells, no chatting or any
sounds, just quietness as everyone was just
staring at him in disgust, and disbelief. He
was in a puddle of an excrement, a stench
that was awful, from his last nights pig
feet dinner. And this afternoons buffet all
over the floor. The whole casino was quite,
and just staring at him. He was still
yelling, and screaming he won, and after a
moment or two he finally took the shock out
of himself, and looked around, and then
looked at the Spinerator 711, and realized

he didn't win. And was full of pooh, all over himself. With his pants all the way down filled up with excrement's. Daryl looked up with disbelief, and then the very last person Daryl ever wanted to see, was right in front of him, Jessica. Jessica said.

" I guess you were right about saying what you told me in the past about you being the shit. And now I will be sure to tell everyone what I saw, and will testify that you truly are the shit, and thanks for not giving me any of your shit."

Daryl was so embarrassed, seeing that everyone was recording with their cell phones and uploading it to the Internet. Daryl ran away falling down since his pants were really low making him trip with excrement splashing all over the surrounding area, and some fecal fragments flew, and hit whoever was near. All the senior citizens there around him got drops of wet diarrhea, and some in line were with disgust of what was happening. Some started to vomit. Some were yelling, and saying.

"Pull your pants up boy, and go get diapers. Did your mommy pack you extra drawers? You really are the shit. Why aren't you a potty-trained boy? Man you made the Spinerator 711 have shit all around it, get a belt you fool."

And many other comments till Daryl left the building.

A senior citizen in the Spinerator 711 line said.

"Its OK boy, I think I need to
change my diapers too. Darn long line."

Daryl was terrified, and embarrassed
since this all happened. He vowed to never
return to this casino again. The Devil was
inside his head now from all the fear, and
hatred he had on the people in the casino.
As he went into the public bathroom. Some
11-year-old boy said.

" Ha ha you're not potty trained.
Like me."

Daryl was furious, and beat up the
kid excessively, then grabbed him, and made
the kid drink from a dirty toilet.

Daryl ran out of the casino, and
into the street, where he was hit by a
moving truck. The truck killed him on
impact.

After time, Daryl is judged and sent
to the Super Nova, for eternity.

CHAPTER TWELVE

FELON K-BOX ARENA Y=0..0='s

Back at the Gate of Realms, a man
by the name of Steve, appears in the
court yard, and asks Saint Peter a bizarre
question.

"Why was the Anti+Christ chosen to
be the Anti+Christ?"

Saint Peter said.

"Revise your visions."

Then the cloud moistened an image,
showing the occurrences, that led him to be
who he is now.

The year is 2033.
Mike Angelo goes live.

"We are live with Olivia Delacruz,
near a prison house, retaliation that has,
just occurred. Olivia, inform us, of the
breaking development, that is happening,
over there, this evening."

"Olivia Delacruz, reporting live, with breaking news. A fire and, riots are going on, in a prison house, here in Mayami, Florido. The prison house, has been taken over by the inmates. The Police are estimating, that about 300 convicts, some inmates, being cold-blooded killers, have escaped this evening. Most of these inmates, did not have the death penalty sentence. But there were about 200 inmates, which have life sentences, and some of those inmates, have two consecutive life sentences.

These inmates, are ruthless, and desperate. Authorities are cautioning the public, that these inmates overtook the prison house armory. Took some weapons, and ammunition. The public is warned, to be cautioned, to lock their doors, and windows, till further notice. The Police, are

advising, that the inmates might be armed,

and dangerous. That the public, needs to

lock all doors, and use any national

security, safety measures to protect their

residence. Police told, the public, to stay

away from the area if possible, and proceed

with caution, if you're in the area."

As Olivia's, eyes, open widely and

continues reporting, in her flashy, red

suit. She was emotionally displaying,

herself, with sadness.

"We have just confirmed that there

in fact, were picketers, picketing here this

morning for the humanitarian life choice.

These picketers were protesting THE FELON K-

BOX ARENA matches. The picketers, prefer to

not give the death penalty to any inmates,

and allow them choice of life, to trust in
reform, and repent before it is too late.
Their goal is to stop the death penalty, and
ironic as it might be, they do not believe
in the Devil.

However, the picketers, were
confronted, by some of the escaped, inmates,
and have abducted, at least five woman
picketers. I was just informed, and the
picketers leader of, Christ Against The
Death Penalty LLC, was also abducted. She
was the first to be taken as hostages, and
there were teens, among the crowds
picketing. The Police chief said there have
been 20 other picketers, not accounted for,
and is believed, to be in the prison house
as hostages.

The Police are advising the public to not open their doors, to anyone, till the pack of inmates, are stopped, and captured. The police, FBI, special forces, Swat, coast guard, army, have, quarantined, the area and, will be squeezing the perimeters, till all are captured. The service men have orders, and permission, to kill on the spot, as all the escaped inmates now have the death penalty, if any bad altercations occur, while being captured.

We will go back to a short commercial break. I will keep us all informed, as new developments occur, and so far there have been seven fatalities reported. This is Olivia Delacruz reporting live, back to you, after this announcement from our sponsors."

A commercial is heard, and the singing begins by saying.

"Mega Megatastic, cola is so yummy, yummy sola, cola yummy yummy cola is caffeine cola, yummy yummy cola, drink it every day, yummy yummy. Go, and power up, and buy my yummy yummy Mammi for my tummy, yummy yummy, for my tummy, yummy yummy, Mega, Mega, Mega, Mega, Mega, cola, Mega, Mega, Mega, Yummy, Megatastic colaaaaaaaa."

Michael says.

"Back on air, Please continue Mr. Governor Washington."

The Governor, of the State, begins to explain.

"If any inmate posing as a family,
and try to hinder this investigation in any
shape or form, we will make you into an
accessory to the crimes. We are trying to
catch a murdering rapist, who in fact will
be found with your co-operation or without.
You are aware that if you are against this
investigation. We, will hold you in
contempt, and if any of your cousins or
siblings are involved, and you're against
this new policy means you are hiding
something. Therefore, by you hindering the
investigation makes you an accessory to the
crime. Your actions criminalize themselves,
and you are now part of the sanctioned Court
Order.

Warranted, for us to capture all
criminals, for the new evaluation al,
justice system. Too finally, do the proper

elimination process. Illuminate the
criminals, and make them pay for their sins
to society, and God's laws. If this criminal
comes into your home, and kills, and rapes
you or your family, is that OK? Should this
be blamed on you? We found female DNA, with
the registered criminals DNA. In all the 10
homes they invaded, and with the same group
of DNA, in all locations.

There are terrorists, in your
communities, and the inmates seem to be
working, with unwilling, or UN-witty female
hostages. As this is a multi task operation
of criminals, and we have quarantined, this
community, to find this family of
terrorists. We have captured most of the
criminals. But have about 30 unaccounted
for.

You can co-operate, and we can do,
and process your DNA, here or at your home.
If you say you are, whom you say you are.
You will have nothing to worry about. We
have quarantined, the whole City. We will
quarantine the whole state or Country if we
have to. Now it is just a matter of time
before we catch all of you, escapees.

Or, we can go to the station, and
have the court-ordered sample. There is a
large waiting list for the Magistrates to be
seen, so you will be held in contempt of the
court order, and held in the waiting
facility to see the Magistrates. We are at
War in our own Country, and we have a weapon
to capture this inhumane crowd of Felons."

So the communities started a new
Filing system, to fight, inter Country

Border Closure. Those inside the new borders of integrated safe border Closure were welcoming border growth to members of society that followed regulations for family growth for God.

This new community grew quicker among the neighboring cities, and merged together with Countries, to get into the world network filing system to capture the notorious criminals, and border against Countries that opposed the border regulations. We are only going to eliminate the guilty, as there will be no more hiding. As eventually, they will be found, and titles will be issued to families, so they can never be fraud-ed again, by this new filing system.

Governor Washington continues.

" Those, which oppose, will be considered terrorist groups against the cause. Since they have, something, to hide. The humans, who do not, register, must have done something in the past, and are hiding. We will be mostly interested in those that do not want to register."

All nations, joined slowly, but a small country in Africa.

Governor Washington continues speaking.

"We will work together to become a civilized unity of humans. All other so called, dictators failed because the plan, was not for the people. But when you do it for, The One United Nation For God. We will succeed. The other failed governments failed, because they were in it for the greed, and hindered the real progression, a healthy economy is supposed to be, for the people. So it will be successful, everyone gets a piece of the pie.

The tax payers are at prey when there is a corrupt government, taking for their own malicious tender. As the circle of life or economic wheels spin for progression. How fair is the economic turn oil if there will always be a loser, dying at the hospital, from not having any form of rejuvenation?

That person may have been a person, who bumps, peoples auras, to make some avalanche of a world of difference. If the government does not have a progression plan

in place then they have failed, for all
their future generations. All our Grandest
Grand children, will be the ones to suffer.

Our government must take the
leadership to harness the contemporary world
we live in, and vastly. BLESS THE PEOPLE
THAT WORKED THE HARVEST, in the past. As now
robots, will be doing, all the food
gathering, and growing. The clock is
ticking, and we will find all of you scum,
that escaped the prison."

Michael now, continues.

"Thank your Governor Washington, for
that insight, and if anyone has seen, them
or if you are out there, and are tired of
running. Call us at our hot line. Anonymous
if you would like, to be. But help, your

community, take these, violent, people off the streets. Peaceful communities, is the way it should be."

The interview continues, with the so called, Anti+Christ. Michael is back live on air.

"Good day, people of this planet. We have a guest on video chat, which we have been waiting for. Yes you guessed it, the one and only Ra. We welcome you today, so enlighten us with, some parables, as you would say is the thing to say."

Ra. thanks Michael, and says.

" As I was indicating the importance of how the molecular structure of the sun is so powerful that it is disintegrating all substances within. Melting Popsicle, and evaporating water into the atmosphere. Then becomes, a new form of melted, and bonded gas into the substances, from the new air molecules host. Imagine what it takes to keep the Sun going.

However, utilizing the same effect, and extending it to a different distance, from the sun, to our Planet. Manipulating, our weather, an atmospheric climate, with total control, of the planets distance, from each other. With the assistance, of this Ancient Alien device. We speculate on closing the circuit of the planet, and completing the Ancient Artifacts, to their original condition or better. To balance the energy, the Sun can do for mankind. Not just, with, solar power. We have to spend the tax payers' money on progression, and

this will give back to the community 10
fold.

An abundance created, by ending
world hunger. By creating natural, food
incubators, by natural and manmade
subterranean green houses, with sun feeding
creation. But, on a mass level. Having
thousands of buildings, above, and
underground for harvesting, all type of
crops. These, AC less obligated formed
mirrors, replicate, or actually transponders
the same sun rays. In a controlled form,
coming from a satellite, that is pointing,
to the Planets location, of Food Plant
Operations. Precisely. Efficiently and, all
year.

Causing dedicated sunlight beams to
power the Planet. The internal sun rays from

the sun can be manifested to underground mines, powering light underground. How the Egyptian's Great Pyramid, functioned, to power up, shooting a direct light beam, within the dedicated passage, on top of the pyramid.

The amazing thing is that the satellite that most people took for granted is still up there in space. The funny thing is we call it a Moon. That is why the Moon has so many holes. The rays come out from the Moons redirect entrances, and power up, certain locations.

These projects are on a humongous level, and I understand, that the people want a guarantee, for this great progression of achievement, to be made. Well I have solved the crises for world hunger, and

these, initial, seven story buildings, will
be created with the money produced by the
public servants. These volunteers, will
help, in aiding the creation of a world
hunger defeater machine.

There are now, underground food
producing factories, enlightened, by these
special mirrors. That brings in the lighted
power, which feeds the sun-lighted power, to
all the stories of the factory. So no grid,
electricity will be needed, and the energy
will be abundant.

And so the obligated mirrors were
made, and indoor farming, have never had
such an abundance for human kind. This type
of food production, could be replicated, on
any planet. The moon already has many of

these buildings ready to replicate the
seeds', we so, sew.

On another note, the acts of
violence are another factor that needs to be
remedied. As those escaped inmates, need to
escape this planet permanently. The urge,
and rage to kill a human being, and take the
life of someone else. Is wrong? The rage is
a time bomb waiting, and ready to explode.
The age of a human mind, receiving life
lessons, either good or bad we proceed to
the next chapters, of ones, own lives, with
multiple possible outcomes. Regardless if
there are casualties? Human life, and so
called, collateral damage, is not in the
equation. Even children or brother or
sisters, are off limits.

We have drafted to legislation, a manner of reform or do not reform policy. It is cut and dry. Either they do or they do not do. Period. We have the reform, with choices. The choices are simple, if they choose, reform, they can prove it, to us. Not just talk the talk. But, walk the walk. We have devised, doorways, with a true choice of reform.

Each doorway entrance was given a name, by mischievous inmates, as only inmates on a death row, was allowed in this hallway. Each room is described as follows.

Door 1. Room one.

Marked with signs: Repentance. Suicides drop. The born loser?

The first door was back to the stairwell of the inmates temporary, holding cell. This deemed the inmate, does not want to fight to the death. And perhaps reform is possible, unless they want to come back, and try again, to see if they, do not coward, out.

Door 2. Room two.

Marked with signs on the wall, of:
The Shitting Room.

The second door was a wash room. In case the inmates had last minute jitters, to use the toilet, or wash themselves. The inmates usually had a very large last, or perhaps a victory meal. They were able to order anything their mind desired to eat. Any meal that was equal to some kings meal, if they desired. This room was made, for the inmate to use the bathroom, and have a last meal.

Signs of statements are posted, around the room, as. Room ponders, and thinks, your choices wisely. There are three more doors to choose from. If I choose 4th door, it is the fight to the death, and I might, be able too win. I will get to see the Winners Mansion, and I will be able to have any thing I desire in the Winners City. Or I can choose Door 1, and walk away. I will not just be walking away. But I will be called a coward, for the rest of my life. Since, I have, a life sentence, and I could be alive, for many more years. But, with the memory, of a coward. That is part of reforming, humbling yourself, and serving

others. What will the inmate, decide? Reform
or fight?

Door 3. Room three.

Marked with signs, on the wall, of:
Good vs. Evil.

24 hours cool off room. So be it.
The 3rd doorway led into a meditation room,
with pictures, and images of Heaven like
pictures, and images of what Hell, may look
like. As, life gives us choices of good or
evil. This psychological test was, to
understand the choice of the human. Either
influenced, by Demons or Good Angels. The
mind is blank with thoughts of nothing,
until thoughts images of equal values
influence the thoughts of humanity. This
waiting room, was unlocked, and inmates were

aloud to stay in there for 24 hours, before deemed a loss. There were plenty of food, and refreshments, for last meals, or first of many more good meals to come for the winner, in this room.

These, 24-hour cool off period was the inmates' last chance to see if they truly were acceptable, for interacting with certain communities. Or if they were good for the death penalty. The next door might bring that fate. Now the jury is out, but there is no judges, or anyone else to influence the humans' thoughts. In normal everyday communities, access to images, of evil or good thoughts are available for anyone to look at, may it be on paper or digital media. However, if the thoughts are simple, and the human journeys, through life knowing there is good, and evil everywhere.

Even more accessible to anyone from the Internet. But it is each human in communities that have to act accordingly to society. So if the human is influenced good or bad, then that is their choice.

So be it. 24 hours cool off room. Now, if the inmate decides that they are, eager to kill. Their choice of charity, and, or families will receive the donation lump sums of money, for the broadcast-ed fighting, and killing other wanted felon inmates, were permitted. More donations accumulate greater, for hated fighters. Especially, felons, of heinous crimes, had large donations. For the victims, friends or families, that had, thirst for revenge, will be displayed. The felon criminals, opened up, and agree to punish more, or be punished. They decided that it is time, but to be the greatest fighter displayed for 2 minutes, or 7 days, in history. Then the inmates are allowed to enter the next door, within the 24-hour period.

Now if the inmate declines to fight, they may go back to their cells, within the 24-hour period. It is the choice of each human to get to this time in their life to explode, or not. May it be in this controlled arena or in the public next to other humans? The timer in the head of a human is set to go off regardless what you do. The clock is ticking, and the human will erupt that year, that month, that day, that second, and boom. It happened. The historical, tragedy. If the humans are recruited in time, then they will be in a controlled environment, with charities winning, and allowing what will occur to occur against their chosen adversaries. Each fighter is allowed to fight exclusively against their hated cause. May it be bias, prejudicial, hatred, political motivated, religious callings, they deemed, they had to be there to do it, or just because they were bored? Whatever the case. The felons, may choose, their fate.

Door 4 Room Four.

Marked with signs of: Big Boss Winner! Oh Yea! Oh Yea!

The fourth, and final doorway is into a Plexiglass elevator, that takes them to a conjoined room, that is the size of a football field, but caged in. Drones are everywhere, for every angle view, recordings. If one of the fighters wanted to run around, and tire the other fighter, they

could. These fights were scheduled until

death, which may be a week if necessary. But

a fair, one on one fight. Or a gang of

fighters. If the talker talks too much, the

wind might hear his wishes, and vibrate the

existence of the talker becoming the walker.

The arena of choice, and/or certain death,

was lit up with symbols of $$$$ in

fluorescent lighting. This door entrance is

where the fight to the death will be

broadcast-ed to the planet. Now if the

inmate decides not to fight. This might be

their last opportunity to fight. If the

inmate, enters, and changes their mind, and

the other fighter inside room 4, decides not

to fight. Then the game is a draw, and no

one wins any prize. This is unlikely to

happen, as no inmate would, refuse to fight.

According to the interviews, done with the

inmates, they can, not wait to donate the
cash prizes to their siblings. But normally
if a fighter shows, signs of being a coward,
it enrages the other fighter more, seeing
the fear of the coward, in a real fight to
the death. It was, some bullies, paradise.

If the inmates wanted to fight with
weapons on a small scale, of acceptable
weapons, then the inmates were allowed to
both use equal weapons. If an inmate was
brave, and fearless, they would allow, the
opposing inmate to choose a weapon, or fight
without a weapon. Again it is their choice
to fight or not. Either way, both inmates
that entered room 4, and closed the locking
door behind them would get the prize money
gifted to their chosen charities. As long as
one of the inmates were killed, or executed
per say. If both inmates, died, then it

becomes a winning draw, and the wining, and

losing, prize money, is given to both, the

deceased chosen, favorite charities. Most

inmates, which were parents, donated the

money to their children or family members.

As this was the greatest gift of money that

would be donated to their children, or

families. As some of the criminals who

fought in a life time of robberies would

never accumulate so much money, as to fight

for a cause greater than their lives,

itself."

Michael says.

Just in! We have a caller, saying

the location of the leader of one group of

gangs. This information has been passed to

local authorities in the area. I believe

Olivia is close to the area. Let us, patch

her in, and, see if there are, any facts, to
this caller."

Olivia Patches in with the callers,
and says.

"We are limited on the Internet in
this area, but Police are on the scene, and
it appears, like they are taking out a body
bag that has been confirmed to be the leader
Steve, from the Notorious Mocos 88 gang.
Police are asking us to leave the area,
since they will be attempting to capture the
rest of the escapees. Will update, the
latest, as soon as we know more. Back to
you, Michael."

Steve's soul, is then vacuumed out of, The Gate of Realms, and sent to the Nova Sun, to fuel more Galaxies.

As the Grapevines of souls disengages another Ovarian Grape fish like cell, and a Young man by the name of Richard, is released into The Gate of Realms.

Saint Peter, greets Richard Ramiro. Richard, says.

Why am I here? Is this a dream?

A vision starts in his mindless soul.

The year is, 2066, mid October.

"In our first fight for tonight we
have Carl Smithsonian, a man who was
incarcerated for 70 years for murder of his
co-workers, and other murders, that were
never proved, but thought by investigators
he did it. But because Carl is a man of his
word, he told investigators he would
disclose all his crimes, if THE FELON K-BOX
ARENA, would be permitted. More inmates not
just Carl, voted the system to be. If
certain criminals, gave up information of
details of all, unsolved felonies, and
crimes that the inmates were convicted for.

In return for being honest, the
inmates got a ticket, to riches, in THE
FELON K-BOX ARENA. The truth was told, so
the victims could have closure. Some of the

past, recent victims of Carl, from his
office, were killed, for just not saving him
any dough nuts in the past. That was the day
Carl finally cracked. We interview him now,
as he explains why he is in here, now."

        Carl says:

    " This thing, is it on? Oh, wait, I
can hear myself. Let me turn it down. OK.
Well, where do I begin? Well, I killed my
first victim because he was annoying me, and
he owed me money. I lent my neighbor, whom
was a dirt bag, some money, and let him
borrow five dollars for, a sandwich. My
neighbor Ron, said he would pay me back that
same day. But never paid me back. I did not
see him, for two days? I got tired of
waiting because I wanted to buy a sandwich
with that $5. I gave him. I reckon then,

since he told me he was not going to pay me back, and laughed, like I was his little puppy. We were in my backyard, when I was having a BBQ. I turned the other cheek, and let it slide.

He had the nerve to ask me, to invite him for dinner. He whistled at my daughter in her bathing suit, and disrespected her, and called me a Punk. I think that is what really ticked me off. Sure, your welcome to eat with me, if I like you. OK, you disrespect me, is one thing. But, now you disrespect my daughter. It is over. So, I smashed, and caved his head in, with my bare fists. After he was dead, I kept hitting him, since I was already looking at brains, on my hands, and that made me madder, that I had his yucky brains, on my hands. His cat, came into my house, where I dragged his wasted body, in the room. That stupid cat, started eating his brains. I got mad at him, so I grabbed the cat, and put him in the microwave, for 3 minutes. Sure I got away with that murder, but I was upset my daughters had to see that."

As Carl dazed, smiled, and laughed, since he thought it was funny in his vision as follows:

" The microwave didn't kill whiskers the cat in 3 minutes, so I put it in for 10 minutes, and the cat cooked, and boiled to death. It was ssssooooo funny. After, thinking what the cat was doing, by eating his owners brain, gave me an idea. I grabbed my butcher knife, and BBQ-ed my neighbor, and cat. Gave most of the meat to my dog. I

was not to keen, on eating diseased flesh.
He did ask me to invite him for dinner, so I
did. Ha ha ha ha.

     Some people just annoy me, and when
they annoy me I feel like I should kill
them. I respect woman, and children, and
hate the convicts in here that are in here
for violating, or raping women or children.
I killed the guy, which I use to share my
cell with, just for that reason. I would
have eaten all of him but the guards stopped
me, since he tasted like poo, uncooked. He
had so much, excretion, in his belly. I
gagged, and could not eat him anymore. My
cell mate, was a child molester, and had the
nerve to kill his own Mother, his own
Mother. That is what I am disgusted with the
most. His own Mother? What the?

The cell mate was bragging about doing it, and almost getting away with it. I was beginning to get annoyed, by him by bragging about how he killed his own, 60 years old, mother, and molesting his little sister, for more then two years. I snapped, and grabbed him, and threw him on the floor, and said, how do you like this, Mother killers? Choking him, that evening, and, feeling good, about doing it. Like as, if I was told, by God, himself, to kill this idiot. I know I saved the tax payers money for 20 or more years.

This guy bragged how he beat the system by having a good lawyer, and how he planned on getting out in five years with good behavior. I thought how do you like your lawyer now? That got you shorter time then you thought. Ha. I'll bet my cell mate never thought he was going to get out of prison this fast. Hahaha. While I have a 70, year sentence, from a public defender, and that irritated me, off, even more. When this scum bag told me, he was going to get out in five years. So I let my poor cell mate's soul out that night. Hahaha. Well you could say I was his Judge, and he was dismissed from the prison holding for life. Hahaha.

This dead inmate here is going to get out probably 10 years, and go, and molest another, little kid, and probably kidnap the kid, while I am still in prison. I have two kids myself, one child is four, and the other is seven years old, and I don't care if I have more time on my sentence. I am a man of my word, and I will tell you. I will kill again, if I was let out tomorrow, and went out in society, I would kill someone, not premeditated but out of a whim. I belong in here, I will kill forever if I could. A vigilante in a way, you may say. Heck some of the victims offered me some nice gifts for my kids if I kill Richard Ramiro. Heck I would kill him for free. But, hey I am not going to, say no, to my kids, and family living outside of this cage. I'm not a dead beat dad anymore, I am going to provide for my family, being locked up in here by doing something I love to do.

If I do not get to fight in the arena, there will be riots, and deaths' greater then these single life sentence inmates. The tax payers, will have to pay more revenue, for medical injuries, and then the law suits, that will form from the on going riots, that will come from all inmates

in here for 70 years to life. That's a small
population, and then there will be the bad
assess that will want to come in here to
fight, to take care of their families, in
prison by these fights. They will make more
money for their families or charities, in
these fights, then on the streets. The tax
payers have nothing to lose, and true
victims will get their true justice. Of
course if their opponents, do not win.

I'm going to kill anyway. I'll go
after any ethnicity, terrorists, rapists,
killer. Bring them all. If they are low life
scum touching one of my kids, I will kill
them. I won't stop. This is the first time,
I could provide, for my family, if I win, or
lose. I feel I can control my rage, if I can
explode in THE FELON K-BOX ARENA. I will
contain the rage, and let the clock start

before I release it, just thinking of those criminals out in the street, that could hurt my family."

As Carl snouts his nose, spits on the ground, and continues.

"If they are convicts that deserve to die of my standards, I will kill them. This event that Ra., or Ka, or whatever his name is, has established something that will save many innocent lives, and bring real justice in a new perspective. These events will tame society, and alleviate the bad from the good. Most of the inmates here are liars if they say they will never kill again.

Once you have tasted the sweet taste of a justifiable kill, life is never the

same. You can't forget it, ever. Especially,
if the kill was someone you hated so much,
that brings a vigilante justice. Everything
is now legal in these events. There is no
heart in these fights. I am going to perform
on these challengers, and my rage I need to
dismiss. I will fight anyone that fights me.
I will literally bite their balls off, and I
will take their eyes out, or do whatever, it
takes to win. Not just for the extra
privileges, which I am going to receive, if
I, win. Or the extra pack of smokes, and
drugs, that I get if I win. I can't wait.
But some of these guys I will fight, and
kill these people for free.

I'll whip their tush for good, and
permanently. I know the victims families
will send me extra presents, because I will
do what the justice system fails to do, by

reforming these guys. Anyway. Any disrespect is all it takes. These fights will save millions, for all the destruction, that some inmates, do in their cells or the pain, or killings that some inmates do to officials, or other inmates, for harm, that is committed. And what happens?

The tax payer has to pay more, for the extra years that the inmates get while in prison. Bring on the fights, it will let out a lot of stress, on some of us here, and the fights will generate more money, from the live on demand broad casts. Of course, this is not for the faint at heart. But I guarantee that the victims of the inmates, will be watching the fight, and feel more that justice is being done, by the pain being inflicted on the perpetrators. Unless, they lose, of course. I can't say it will help, the victims' family that I hurt, but it's better then nothing.

So many inmates have died fighting in the prisons, and there was no benefit for anyone really. With this system, it will bring back society, to a new reform. Criminals will die out, and become extinct, but real criminals that are violent, will come to prison, and take the rage out, and love it here. As their true home, and burials, for all the losers, that crossed the wrong path. They are home.

I'll tell you, I can't wait to go in the ring, and kill again, and be a triumph. If I die fighting, I won't care since I was on a death role anyway, after I killed my cell inmate. I can't wait to go to the ring. Ever since the ring matches got scheduled.

There has been a new code in here. No
inmate, has fought anymore. It's now called.
Save it, for the ring. All inmates will not
cross the line, and fight. We all know
whoever breaks. Save it for the ring, rule,
will get killed, and their families will get
visitors from not so friendly people. Dumb,
Bozo last year broke the rule, he got jumped
by everyone, even the prison guards jumped
in, and helped kill the bastard. 270 day
streak of nonviolence in the cell blocks,
across the countries, and the world. Gone.
For some dumb ass getting disrespected. He
could have, manned up, and said let's settle
this, in THE FELON K-BOX ARENA. Like a real
man, of his word.

We finally made it to our first
fight, and I'm so excited I can't wait. Even
though, that Senator or lady Judge. Whatever

her name is, Gumenheimer thought since, all inmates have been so fantastic, and good in the prison systems, that humans could be controlled, and reformed. That we did not need the fights anymore. That we were better off without violence. That if the inmates could control, not to fight for a record breaking number of an exact year.

We did it for 365 days, as the court order had agreed, for us to be able to have these fights, to be legal. She canceled it all. She said, that gifts were still allowed to be given to inmates, but no fights would occur, or be legal. She went back on her word!

The next day as soon as they let the inmates out of our cells, all the inmates attacked, and killed rival enemies, security guards. You name it they got killed to. They took picketers from the front of the prisons. I knew this was going to happen. So I went immediately to John Helms. He was going to be, one of the persons I was suppose to fight, and kill on live TV. So I went, and slowly killed him, the next day. When Congress, changed the order, for the fights, not to exist, the mayhem commenced. There was much violence. Some of the family, and Congress members were killed. Congress really had no choice but to allow history to take place. The Congress changed the order of the fights. To permit, the fights, to be, legal venues. The fights, were now, legalized for the world wide gambling, arena.

That same week after all the dilemmas, I remember a little girl that reminded me of my own daughter. She visited me in prison, but she was no more then 16 or 17. Her name was Johanna. The prettiest, little girl, I had seen, in a very long time. I was thinking the guards, confused me, with someone else."

The guardsman said:

"Nope, this is correct, and she asked for you specifically."

Carl continues:

"I asked the little girl if there was something I can help her with?"

Johanna said with big green eyes looking up at him, and started.

"Are you Carl who is in here for
life that is Scheduled to fight in THE FELON
K-BOX ARENA?"

Carl said.

"I told her, yes, and what may I do
for such a pretty flower like herself."

Johanna had tears in her big green
beautiful eyes, and said.

"Please. Mister? If you say no, I
will understand. My Mom, and Dad use to rent
a room, to a cousin, that lived with us for
five years. He would rape me once or twice a
week for five years straight, and he gave me
A.I.D.S.. I was told I will probably not
live past my 21st birthday, according to

doctors. Richard told me that he would kill my parents if I told anyone.

When my parents confronted him, he killed both of them, and took me with him, saying he would take care of me, till I was dead. I ran away as soon as I got the chance. I feel like dying every day, I know he's still alive. He was captured, years later, but murdering a lot of people, while he was on the run. There is nothing I have, that I can give you, except, a great, thank you, appreciation, and my teddy bear that gives a lot of love. But, I was wondering if you could fight Richard Ramiro?"

Carl raises his hand, and says.

"Say no more little princess. I will take care of it for free. Or, well, if maybe, you can visit me, once a year, or write to me, letting me know, you are OK. That's all I ask. Since, no one, ever visits me, anymore. Since my daughters, saw me, kill a man, in front of, their pretty, little eyes. I understand, that they would never want to see me again. I think of my friends, and family, but they do not think of me. I will take care of him for good, so you know he will never harm you or anyone, again. I will request the fight. If he fights me, I will take care of him, little princess."

Carl's eyes are watery, and are saddened, that he knows she is going to die from this idiot, giving her a killer disease.

Johanna starts crying, hugs, and holds Carl.

Carl's eyes, are watering, reminiscing, and continues.

"So after the Congress declined the fights. The next day I got out of my cell, and knew the fights were off. I had nothing to lose, and my little new friend Johanna, will be so happy, her parent's killer, was dead. So if no fights were going to occur, then I was going to make it happen. I ran looking for Richard Ramiro in his cell. While I was holding a make shift shank, I made, with hardened plastic forks, and straws. But Richard was not to be found that day. Instead I saw my other rival enemy, John Helm. I yelled his name, and stuck both shanks up these idiots' nostrils, and into his brains. It paralyzed him, and then I just choked him to death. I felt so glad he was dead, since this jerk, deserves to go to the sulfuric lakes of fire.

The next few weeks went by, and finally, order came with a price that was high to the tax payers pocket books. Death toll rates, came out, to more than 100 dead, and about 10,000 injured. The law suits immediately came, and the lady Judge's ruling, was over turned by Judge Lynch. He has balls, he turned it over as soon as the hostages, or some crap in Southern Califia, prison house, was settled. Some humanitarian hostages that got taken during the commotion. After, all those issues, were settled, the hostages were released, and, here we are. No Judge on the planet, can go against the ruling, of a world militia in a

moment notice. Our communication technology,
got so advance, that mankind, could be
rioting up, for good causes, of changing the
world. Planet, peace follows.

          Another reason we are being
cooperative is that, (Save it For The Ring).
Because, the winner gets rewards, drugs, a
guarded walk on the beach, men or woman
slaves, per say. So inspiring. The
excitement of the fights, to really be
happening. The final releases, of the
captives. It's amazing, but I can't wait.
The Warden will give us anything, except our
freedom, but some of us are home. So were
just getting perks. Some of the inmates,
that only have a few months in here also
want to go in the ring. Just to kill people
they don't like, and it's legal, in that
ring, to do. The inmate will not get

increase time since they fought in the ring, instead of fighting in the prison house of the Warden. Respect was now earned.

The Warden has made it so, and the non felon, gets released in a few months after they do their time. Even after a new murder, of an inmate, but, followed the Wardens rules, was released of liability. The Wardens reason, is that, if an inmate, can control themselves, not to fight in public society, and control violence to only the ring, then those inmates may be released after they serve their time. Now, mind you, most of the contestants are life time, so that will be their permanent home.

The Warden makes, a load of money, if they fight in the ring. It is controlling violence, to a monitored facility, getting

rid, of violent individuals, off the street.
It's a win, win, situation, for everybody,
especially, the tax payer. I was still
hoping that Richard Ramiro, would not change
his mind. So I can take, a chance, on
destroying that killer. The Warden, is still
trying to allow, victims to come off the
street, and fight their perpetrators. With
the app, you can choose your opponent, has a
calendar, with the count down before, the
scheduled fight. Some fights may be
scheduled a year away. But the app keeps you
up to date. It is part of the reform,
process, to be patient and wait it out, or
change your mind.

        The felons, that can not wait, and
want to battle it out that same day, may. An
emergency broadcast is set out to everyone's
app, about the scheduled, 24 hour fight, to

be. Technology. I tell yea. Those fighters,
that have no reform, can cross their path on
the controlled area. The bets go wild, when
one of these fights go out on 24 hour
notice. Some of those fights last less than
15 min. But the line seems to still be long.
Who knows how less of a population, the
planet will have, if the rage keeps up.
Normally the cash prizes are less, for the
24 hour guy. They just want to kill, and are
not in it for the money, anyway. The other
controlled fights are 3 month to a year. I
am a patient man, so I will wait till we are
scheduled, to do my dirty work. Ha ha ha.

They have approved street fighters,
which would have murdered each other, in bar
fights. Those type of fighting matches, are
now allowed to also fight in the ring.
Making money, for fighting in the ring

opposed to, fighting in the street, and being busted, and having to pay restitution. The bar fighters sign a waiver, which if they are not allowed to fight in the ring, their rage may abrupt violence, and innocent public humanity might take a toll. Hence, the bar fighters sign the waiver to be televised, and the survivor walks with $5,000,000. Immediately, in their pocket books application. Like the one I have in my hand. Then the transfer, immediately goes to their siblings.

Again it is a win, win, situation, tax payers save a ton on police investigations, unknown homicide, manhunts that would cost more in taxes. Not to mention the courts, and jury, and everything else that may of even killed innocent people. This way the fights are controlled

by people who were already set to die by
God's clock.

      But just killed, in a controlled
environment, and the gambling winnings,
without fights being fixed. Since the loser
can't take a dive, but a permanent dive. Ha
ha ha ha ha"

      The reporter asks Carl.

      "If you win, in to-days match,
besides 1,000 cartons of cigarettes. What
else are you going to ask for your reward or
grant?"

      Carl laughs, and says.

      "You can't tell anyone."

Carl laughs, as he is, so excited. Then says.

"I am going to BBQ my victim, and eat him. Just like Richard Ramiro stated, in his interview. He told the world that, he will eat all his victims, that cross his path in, THE FELON K-BOX ARENA. He wants to eat me. I will probably just give his parts to the inmates that I invite, to the mansion.

I'm really going to poop in his mouth, once I kill him, on TV. I can't wait, and it is in the contract. That I will poop in his mouth, as the poo mouth, he is. Hahaha Hahaha."

The reporter continues.

"Well there you have it, ladies, and gentlemen. Carl Smithsonian the one of the first fighter ever to be performed on live television to the death. Both men have the death penalty, and both men have agreed that they waive all rights of life. Both men have agreed, and have no problem fighting to the death, and the winner will still have no money tendency gain, but will have material benefits of packs of smokes, cocaine, alcohol, or even the right to be with some women, or men. As little as it might sound, but some of these inmates do not have any privileges, or family, that will ever visit them, and these benefits, are grand to these winning inmates.

All remaining proceeds, after costs of the productions, will go back to the states, and give back to the tax payers.

This is a great country we live in at this present time. Which now brings us to our next challenger. Please clap your hands or give your finger, and flip off our next contender, a serial killer, Richard Ramiro.

Richard said he did not want to be interviewed again, and just wants to let the public know. That he has the power of the Devil, on his side. His request, if he wins, is to be able, to eat his opponent, on a BBQ. As sickening, as it sounds, he has admitted, that this would not be his first victim he has eaten, this way. All opponent, fighting him, have to agree, to be eaten, if the battle, is lost. Carl, is so sure, that he is going too win, that he said if he loses, he deserves to be eaten. That is why Carl, covered himself, with feces, and has that bad odor, I did not want to mention to him. Just in case, it would piss him off. The match is about to begin."

The announcer of the ring starts.

"Ladies, and gentleman, we welcome you today as history is about to be made. We have the whole world watching, for the first time ever, in this live event that will bring total closure, for many families after this battle. We do not have medical staff, for the loser, but a coroner, to determine the time of death. As this battle fight, is to the death. The weak at heart, and minors, please turn your viewing devices off, and go to bed, as this will not be interrupted, or edited, for this broadcast.

In this corner we have the famous, well-known serial killer, He has been charged with 20 documented killings in the past. But after THE FELON K-BOX ARENA fame exposure, he has admitted to more than 200 killings. All bodies have been accounted for except for 20-25 of the murdered victims. His life sentence, previously documented, that those victims were eaten by our opponent Ernie Richard Ramiro."

The audience boos him, and calls him names. Except a few supporters that were allowed, to do a ritual, for Richard. To summon powers, beyond this realm, and to help him win this battle.

The humming, and instrumental sounds, they use are mesmerizing, as everyone in the audience is quite, and listen to the back chilling seance, they perform. To amp Richards serial killer mind.

After the music stopped, and Richard was let into the Arena Box, the announcer then gets lifted out of there. And introduces, Carl from out of the other side of the Arena Box, since he knew they were going to go at it, like dogs being unleashed from their collars.

"Ladies, and gentleman, I now introduce, Carl the Animal. He was incarcerated here for murder, and got 2 consecutive life sentences after killing his cell-mate."

Three hours pass, and Carl does not show up to his designated spot to fight.

Finally Carl is seen.

"Oh gross, what is that smell? Ewww.
Gross. It is like a leaking sewer line. It
is disgusting. Look, Carl is taking, his
robe off, and he is covered with what looks
like a tar, of some sort. It smells like,
poop. Oh, Lord, he is covered with poop.
What is this ladies, and gentlemen, Carl is
naked?"

Lots of laughs are coming from the
audience that is sitting in cells where the
fighting inmates have no access. A real,
coliseum, cage matches with the Y=O..O's

The Y=O..O's were similar, to little
Demon computer silicone chips, or rather
similar to slimy boogers. A virus, which
would attach to a person. Like the flu, or
Corona Virus, that would, attach, to
another, person. An airborne virus. Once

attached, it vibrates a voice, that shakes vibrational wind molecules, to become an insertion to the host. Most hosts had to do evil to become near the induction wave created by these germ Demons. These slime snot, attached to lung tissue, and their voices could be heard by little brain thoughts. The brain abides or fights to or from the thoughts of the germ. If ingested, by close induction, then death to the host, by the germ, followed. If you resisted, painful headaches would occur, as a side effect. If it became you, then it was your new evil voice inside part of your tissue. A spreading cell cancer, of evil. It is only nurtured by evil thoughts. If you are a good person, you are immune to the virus. But dwells on bad, or evil thoughts, created the welcoming of this virus. Known as, The

Y=O..O='s. One sure symptom, is the host,
would continue to repeat and say, yo.

        The Devils son was in, one of the
viewing audience box, of the live fight,
that day, and started a chant.

        O-Yoo Yoos, yell the name, O-Yoo Yoos.
Joo Jooo Yell the name Yoo Yooos.

        Yoooooooooooooooooooooo, oooooooooooo, yo
yo yo, yooooooooooooooooooooou, oo, yo yo yo,
yoooooooooooooooooooooooooo, o yo yo yo,
Yoooooooooooooooooooo, oooooooooooo, yo yo
yo, yoooooooooooooooooooou, oo, yo yo yo,
yoooooooooooooooooooooooooo, o yo yo yo,
Yoooooooooooooooooooo, oooooooooooo, yo yo
yo, yoooooooooooooooooooou, oo, yo yo yo,
yooooooooooooooooooooooooooo, o yo yo yo,

Yoooooooooooooooooooooo, ooooooooooo, yo yo yo, yoooooooooooooooooooooooou, oo, yo yo yo, yoooooooooooooooooooooooooo, o yo yo yo,
Yoooooooooooooooooooo, ooooooooooo, yo yo yo, yoooooooooooooooooooooou, oo, yo yo yo, yoooooooooooooooooooooooooo, o yo yo yo,
Yoooooooooooooooooooo, ooooooooooo, yo yo yo, yooooooooooooooooooooou, oo, yo yo yo, yoooooooooooooooooooooooooo, o yo yo yo .
Hrrrreerer, herererreeerer.

    The demonic vibrations for a visual image of a Demon appears, and he yells to the man.

        "Do it so you show you reign, as a man, and kill those around you to get even for the ridiculing, and the bullying that humans did. Have a reservation with our elite group, which will show you, the way to riches, you never could of imagined."

So Richard, complied, and knew he was doing something wrong in the back of his mind. He remembered all the good he had, growing up, and all the good memories he had with his family around him. He was in the cross hairs, of his biggest decision in his life.

This man could be anyone but this was the guy who never thought it could be him. His life was now over if he made the wrong decision.

The announcer continues.

"Carl is funny, and he is running into the 4th Door and into the elevator plexiglass Box. He is not wasting anytime as he jumps inside, and the security guards lock up the box doors, to get the fight started. Carl runs, and hits Richard in the jaw knocking him down, and it looks like the poop is getting all over the place, even on Richard. Richard's face is very upset, and looks as if he is gagging, from the smell Carl has smothered on him.

Carl is not being merciful, as he really wants too win this match with no rules, as he knows his opponent will BBQ his body, if he loses. Richard is no match for Carl's strategy, and is being held in a hold by the animal Carl. Richard has just grabbed Carl's genitals, and one of them is turning blue.

Richard has extremely long nails he grew to scratch Carl's eyes out, as rumors had said. Carl should have worn a jock, to this battle, as I think, there might be blood. Wow it looks like Richard has just, popped out, one of Carl's eye sockets.

There is something else coming out of Carl. Oh no he didn't, but oh my goodness it is. Carl is squirting out feces from his butt, and it looks like Carl is grabbing, his own feces. The smell is horrendous. I can't believe this is going on right now.

Richard bites Carl, right in the face. It looks like he may have bitten a piece of flesh off Carl. Richard is now gagging, and looking away, as Carl rams the big turd, that just came out of him into Richards mouth. Richard is gagging.

Oh no, he just vomited all over, on Carl. Carl is still trying to suffocate Richard. Richard is still vomiting all over. Richard, does not look good. Carl is choking him as, still injecting feces down his mouth. This is upsetting my stomach as I have never seen anything like this.

Richard now looks lifeless, with poo, all over his face. Literally, you could say. He did get poo faced, before he died. Carl now gets up runs up, and down, knowing he just won. What is Carl doing now, it looks like Carl just bit off, Richards nose, and he is smiling.

Now Carl is looking a bit sick, and has also, just tossed his cookies. What a match ladies, and gentleman. As the crowd is going wild, and the victims of Richard have finally gotten closure. Carl is cheering, and we will get an interview from him in just a bit, after that guy showers, and medics help him.

If these were round fights, the fight lasted around 1 round. Ladies, and gentleman. One round, and was killed in 4 minutes flat. Look. There goes Carl, trying to now poop on top of Richard's head. He has no more poop. He is trying, but nothing is coming out.

As 10 minute passes, and still nothing comes out of Carl. This is humiliating for Richards supporters. Wait, wait here goes Carl it is a little piece he finally got out of him. Amazing what Carl is capable of. He pooped on his opponent as he said he would do. We will talk to him after he gets medical aid, definitely showers, and cleans himself. As he is still alive, he will get medical treatment for his injuries, as his opponent was officially pronounced dead, by the coroner. FELON K-BOX ARENA, winners will always be taken care of, to fight another day, if they wish. Amazing match. Just an amazing match."

As Carl enters his new home, for the first time, and is ready for an interview. Carl, begins yelling he won, limping a bit, with crutches, from his genital injuries. He enters the winners, multi roomed, mansions, freshly showered, with a big smile. And says.

"I told you, I told you, I would do it, I told you I would. I am a man of my word. I may be a thief, a murder, all the bad things you can think of, but yes it is true I am a man of my word. Just like in the Bible, you make a promise you keep it, no turning back, you say it, you do it. I live in this Mansion now, and I get mass drugs now. Where are my drugs that I was promised?'

An attractive woman enters the room half naked with all the drugs he requested, and a big check that he had to donate to a charity, friends or family that was not incarcerated.

Chuck, the Interviewer begins with.

"Carl that was an amazing, historical fight I have ever seen, in my life. Tell me what were you thinking? What was going trough, your mind, what made you do what you did? Especially, are your balls, OK? He did take a pretty good chunk off your cheek. How are you feeling champ?"

Carl answers.

"My head hurts. My eye, can barely see, from one side. I don't feel like talking now. I will take my drugs, this attractive woman, and go lock ourselves up in my new room in this kick ass Mansion. If you want another interview see me in 3 days. And I would like to, let my Mom know, that she didn't bring up no loser. That she now has a split of the 5 million dollars, from my winning prize money. And Mom, tell my kids that I promise you, and them, there is more money, where that came from.

You know Chuck, I also want to say I feel good, I got that itchy rage out of my system, and I killed a serial killer. I know I am no Saint. But, at least I killed a guy that deserved it, saving society from him doing any harm. His own admission, as well as mine. We can not stop, this itchy rage, we have inside us. But it feels good to let it out, and no innocent person was injured in our battle. I will see you in 3 days Chuck. I am going to my Mansion now. Before you ask. I could not eat this nasty guy, That is sick. If he was going to eat me if he won, then he would of been eating my poo. I could not eat him. Heck I won, why am I going to eat, that piece of poo, when I can eat flame Mignon, steaks, ice cream shakes, cognac, good Jack whiskey and be around better company than him. I was done with him. Do you know how long it would take to cook him? Since now, I can have better than that nasty dead man. I am going to my mansion now, to have a real ready cooked luxury dinner. Good night. I will be back to fight in my already scheduled 3 month tournament. I ate his nose, and kept my word of eating him. It was nasty, the first bite was my last. I will not eat anymore of my opponents. Mock my words on that. Take it to the bank. Lates."

Carl leaves with the biggest smile on his face.

Chuck continues.

"We will be right back, after this announcement, from our sponsors."

A commercial is heard, and the singing begins by saying.

"Mega Megatastic, cola is so yummy, yummy sola, cola yummy yummy cola is caffeine cola, yummy yummy cola, drink it every day, yummy yummy. Go, and power up, and buy my yummy yummy Mammi for my tummy, yummy yummy, for my tummy, yummy yummy, Mega, Mega, Mega, Mega, Mega, cola, Mega, Mega, Mega, Yummy, Megatastic colaaaaaaaa."

"Well just if you did not know the loser does not walk away with nothing. The loser, that died, also, gets 3 million dollars. To be donated to their favorite charity group, family, or friends. As of course, when I say walks away, is not a literal term, but just a saying, as they literally will not be walking away, from the Arena cage.

The next event, will be two lifetime convicts that have shared a life before, they were put behind bars. Our first fighter is a man from Mayrica. By the name of Jeana, and moved here, 15 years ago for the Mericana dream. His dream, interpretation of becoming a drug lord kingpin.

His visions were to take his girlfriends, with him, after completing, all the documents, and paying, all the fees, to get into this country legally. They were admitted by bribes, and after he paid all the fees to pass the tests. Filled out the forms, and came over to this Country. Their first day, they made more than $100,000. Just in drug sales. After 7 years of high

rolling. Their disorganized jealousy,
eventually became, their downfall.

They finally messed up. It all
happened, after Police called out to Jeana's
residence multiple times. So many domestic,
disputes, complaints. Domestic violence, and
rage was hard to control for some people.
And after the 12th complaint, the Police
finally caught them off guard, on the scene.
They caught them red handed, with four dead
bodies, of gang members. Dead in plain site,
in the living room. No search warrant needed
in this case.

The jealous boyfriend, of a
transsexual girlfriend lover, by the name of
Biana. He was so high off heroin that he did
not rationally think of his consequences,
when they got caught. The slaying from the

slow killings, that Biana did to the lovers,
was gruesome. He wanted to keep Jeana for
himself. But that is how the crunchy cookie
crumbles, to all flavors."

        Announcer:

        "And there you have it ladies, and
gentleman, Biana is getting into, THE FELON
K-BOX ARENA. He is getting out of the thick
plexiglass, elevator from Door 4. That Biana
drama entrance performance, and dance are
now in the official fighting box, archives.
Let's, turn, the Microphone, on, it looks
like Biana wants to say something.

        Biana said. With a devilish laugh.

        "I have been poisoned by my enemies
in the past, and I have been poisoned by

infamous characters. Some were, jealous, no
name, motor heads, that did not care about
any consequences. Since they were so high
off reality, that they believed, there is no
God. They thought, they were Gods of who
choose to live, and die. My opponent, is no
different, then any of the other criminals,
that died, and went through roof tops. Or
should, I say, fell off them. You try to
poison Biana and I find out who tried to
poison me, then you will hang. My opponent
the little vanity ditch is out, and will be
put him in the box permanently."

The announcer speaks again:

"Yes ladies, and gentleman here
come, the well known, the underground
kingpin, of Mayano Chincago. He would have
never been caught if the neighbors did not

call of domestic disturbance behavior. The neighbor said, it sounded like people were yelling for their lives. It turns out, they were."

As the announcer covers his nose, since there is a bad smell, from the adjacent doors, that sweep the audiences, main smelling, trigger. The poo hit the ceiling fans.

The announcer continues, and says.

"What the heck is that smell, oh my God, not another, feces, covered inmate. Is this the trend with these guys? This guy is covered all over, with feces. I just can not believe this. He is literally stinking up the place. He is now in the official elevator box. Leaving a trail of poop, right behind him. Where did he get this stuff?

He did say he was having baby back ribs with a whole pig. He requested to eat all of it, as his last meal. They are both in the football field box now, and Jeana is naked. As he knows he is more disgusting, to his opponent, and supposedly, knows he is going too win easily. Since he knows that Biana, is a total clean freak, was going to be so disgusted by the smell, and afraid of such a disgusting act. Biana starts throwing up, falls to his knees, and starts crying.

Now he is throwing up more, as Jeana is laughing there, naked covered in feces from head to toe. He just keeps laughing, looking up, and pointing at the cameras. Knowing he is there with the power to kill again, and breathe in, the poor soul, he once called, Biana, his lover.

As Jeana looks at the cameras, up in the ceilings, and the audience looks up to see what Jeana is looking at. Then he looks, and says.

"You Biana, will bow down to me. I am a soldier, that is placed on this planet, to punish you by death. And all other criminals, that get in my way."

Jeana knows as the winner he will be getting his desperately needed, heroin fixes, for a month, after the match is over. But only after Biana is dead, and terminated from this existence. Jeana, is so excited, too win, and is so sure with his tactics he had planned, will win, as he rehearsed the

exact steps for executing an entertaining
match, for the audiences. In return he will
be getting his heroin fix, for a month,
after every match.

        Jeana even memorized a dance, to do,
a move down crazy groove victory dance. He
was going to call it the new signature match
victory dance by Jeana, that he would
perform, and do after the matches. So the
viewers would choose him, as his ax man for
all matches."

        As Jeana is saying in his mind, and
rehearsing his steps as what he is going to
do to win the match. Biana immediately,
changes his face expressions with hate, and
anger, of the man, that use to be, his
cocaine fix pimp. Biana opens his mouth
strangely, and jumps up, off his knees, and

jumps across to Jeana's waist. And starts to bite off Jeana's genitals, with one quick bite, and without warning.

Jeana was still laughing, and knowing he was going to get a fix, then all of a sudden, he feels the worst pain in his genital area. He looks down, and sees Biana, literally biting off his manhood, down to the edge. Jeana start screaming in pain, and begins to feel light headed as the blood starts squirting out of his veins all over the floor.

Biana is chewing on the flesh covered with feces as if it was a piece of meat. Jeana faints to the ground as the audience is in shock of what just happened, and silence is heard with all the viewers wondering what is going to happen next.

Biana looks at him covered in feces, and blood, and remembers all the good memories of them being together for many years. Biana lays down on the floor, and sticks the remaining manhood by his side, and comforts Jeana with a hug holding him tightly. The audience is still quiet, wondering what just happened? If this was true in amazement.

Biana lays there, and falls slightly asleep in the comfort he feels from all the regret that has happened between them in the past. The crowd is silent as blood is pooling in the box all around the floor. A few minutes go by, and Jeana wakes up light headed, and is wondering if this was a dream.

Jeana then sees Biana with his eyes closed as if in a daze crying softly holding him. Jeana is in a daze, and then looks down as he sees blood all over the place. He remembers, that Biana, bit off his, genital, and was cut off. He sees it is in Biana's side.

Jeana still bleeding, angered, and with a rage gets up, and the crowd goes wild. Jeana grabs Biana's neck, and twists it real hard till Biana could not fight the strength of the rage inserted into Jeana. Biana, dies from his neck being twisted, and broken. The crowd goes wild, and yells Jeana, Jeana, Jeana, as he stands up still light headed, and starts yelling, and screaming he won, and slightly forgets, that he is bleeding all over the place.

As he is feeling faint, and then falls to the ground dying before he hits the ground, from losing too much blood. The match is over, and both convicts are officially dead by the corner. This match seems to be a draw, and was a bust for Vegaz, since none of them really won since both died in the match. There will be no heroin or cocaine for any convicts. Both parties, share the wining and losing funds equally. So a split to both fighters kin, got the winnings.

Biana's soul is thrown into the Sun, to burn for eternity.

Back at the Gate of Realms, a man by the name of Mike, appears in the court yard, and asks Saint Peter the normal questions.

Mike says.

"What just happened? Where am I?"

Then immediately a vision starts:

So Charles James Madison gets out
his Colt 45 revolver, a very limited edition
piece that he had in his collection with a
make shift silencer. He dazes into the gun
thinking deeply wondering if he should
finally go through with killing his wife.

Charles plan is he wanted to kill
his wife to get a very large life insurance
policy that he had placed on his not so
loving wife.

One afternoon Charles went for a drive, and ended up in a blighted part of the city, miles from where he lived. Charles wondered giggling, and thought if maybe he should seek a hoodlum gang member to contract, and get to kill Charles wife.

As Charles is driving around town he sees a man wearing a mask running out of a liquor store running to his buddies, get away car. His buddy Nigel was at the car waiting for him, sketching on drugs, and yelling.

"Hurry up dummy. Lets go!"

Suddenly, 6 loud shot gun blasts are heard, and Nigel is sprayed in the head. Mike is hit in the hand, and causes him to lose his weapon, and 3 fingers. Mike takes

off running, bleeding, and has adrenalin
pumping on high alert. Mike has no where to
run or go. He then gets shot at but missed
and runs quickly away. He is being chased by
the store clerk.

The store owner is trying to reload
more shells into his shot gun. Charles pulls
in front of Mike, and tells him to get in
his car. Mike is in shock, and still can not
believe there are 3 fingers missing. Mike
grabs 2 of his fingers he finds , and jumps
in the car crying and, saying.

"Thanks man. They shot my fingers
off. I did not do nothing."

Charles tells him,

"I am a surgeon, and can help you if you can help me."

Charles speeds away with Mike, and goes to a remote area where it is safe to bandage up Mikes hands. Charles being in the medical field stitches up Mikes hands, and they get to know each other. Mike is grateful for Charles helping him get away.

Charles explains the proposition to Mike, and he accepts.

As Mike tells Charles.

"I am glad, I am still alive. I owe you man, but I'm still going to charge you 60k."

Charles agrees.

Later on as planned on July 4th, at 3 am., Mike breaks into Charles Madison's house, with intent to rob and kill Edith Madison, that evening. Charles was supposed to leave $60,000., for Mikes payoff, on the kitchen counter. Mike was supposed to use the limited edition revolver, left in by the back window, where Mike broke into. Mike was suppose to take sixty thousand, but there was only thirty thousand dollars.

Charles did not realize that his son, Tom had visited earlier that evening, and borrowed $30,000. from his mom. Leaving only $30,000.

Mike was furious that he was shorted on his money, and decided to stay the night, and wait for Charles, so Mike could kill him too. Mike made some sandwiches, and did not care that Edith's lifeless body, was on the floor. There was blood all over the room. Mike did not care at all. He had no remorse, and decided to rape her while she was on the floor dead. Edith was an attractive person, but now her head was mutilated, into a disfigured skull. As Edith use to be a woman, admired by many. Mike then fell asleep, while waiting for Charles.

Charles, prepped up everything, to make it look like, he went downstairs, and found his dead wife Edith on the floor. Charles had a late flight out of the Country this evening, with his Mistress. So he did not want any red tape. So Charles already called the Police, in advanced stating Charles woke up, and found Edith dead. As

Charles walks in, and sees Mike still there
and with the gun pointing at him.

Charles says.

"You have to get out of here, the
police are already coming."

Mike says.

"Nice try buddy. But I am 30k short.
You need to give it to me right now, or I
will shoot you dead."

Charles replies, and yells.

" I am going to need some time to
get it. But if you do not leave right now.
You're going to get locked up, by the
police. They are on the way."

Mike replies.

" I do not like the way you are talking to me, boy. I am just going to shoot you, and squat in this here home."

Charles gets, shot dead. The police are already out front, and hear the shot inside. Backup is called, with SWAT, team. Mike is eventually apprehended.

Tom, the son of Charles, and Edith, wanted vengeance on this man that, killed his parents. Tom signed up, to fight Mike if he accepted to fight him.

Mike liked the idea, of the cash money prize for winner, and thought, if I killed their Mom, and Dad. Then I can surely

kill their son too. I will fight. This
challenge, and live in the Mansion of
winners. I am down he thinks to himself.
Sign me up.

The day for the fight was, finally
scheduled.

Tom exited his fighting chamber, and
went into THE FELON K-BOX ARENA to confront
the felons who killed his parents. Tom was
the son, of the slay-ed victims, and went
into the match, with a small hidden revolver
gun, to kill his parents killer.

Tom's vengeance, was going to be
sweet, and simple. As he was able to payoff
a maintenance worker, to sneak in and bury a
snub revolver, by the 10 yard line.

The plan was simple shoot the bastard that killed his parents, and walk out a free man with the law of voluntary man slaughter in a control environment of FELON K-BOX ARENA. The law was put into effect to maintain criminal activities in a new world order. Tom knew of this, and was allowed to confront his parents killer. Now if the Killer did not want to fight, then the inmate would be allowed to remain in prison, the rest of his sentence.

As this new form of fighting of justice was to stop wars. That any opposing group was allowed to bring their soldiers into battle, in the Control FELON K-BOX ARENA. Terrorist were welcomed, and they could fight, and attempt to kill any opposing soldiers of any group. No more ambushes or secret agendas. If you truly

hate your neighbor, and he hates you back
then relieve the stressful pain in THE FELON
K-BOX ARENA. It is guaranteed to end the
wars of humanity, and instead of having so
many deaths among-st the world. This
alternative, for a better, safer future, of
mankind. The choice is reform, or not.

So Tom exited his Plexiglass,
elevator chambers into the Box, and ran to
the 10-yard line, to sit by the revolver.
Tom waited for his parents, killer Mike. Tom
knew that the inmate has a right, to walk
away and not fight, so Tom could be here for
3 days until, the fight will be canceled or
rescheduled. The inmate may take 24 hours to
enjoy their last meal, before the final
fight. So Tom knew to be patient, as he
meditated that day the longest ever.

After 4 hours of wait. Mike is coming down the elevator, ready to fight Tom. Mikes stomach is very large from eating for the last 4 hours. It was a buffet heaven. The best 4-hour buffet, he has ever had in his life time.

As the elevator door opens. Mike starts running to kill Tom, and is carrying sharpened rib and chicken bones. Also carrying with him, some forks, and butter knives. Of course cheaters never prosper, or do they?

Tom Sees Mike running to him, with an arsenal of possibly, deadly weapons. Tom now has no problem pulling the revolver out, as soon as, Mike is close enough.

Mike gets a close enough range, and starts, shooting 3 times at Mike. Hitting Mike, with 3 fatal shots. Tom goes and shoots Mike one more time in the brain, to make sure, he was dead. Tom is, saddened, that, this kill, was not satisfying as he hoped it would be.

The crowd goes wild, saying Tommy, Tommy, Tommy. Repeating Tommy over, and over.

Tom turns the gun on himself, and shoots himself in the head. Killing Tom instantly.

Mike is then vacuumed, out of The Gate of Realms, and thrown into the Sun.

Both inmates, charities, or next of kin, are giving the prize money equally. As the inmates specified, where to distribute the winnings.

After the fight, the prisons across the nation yell, and scream but stay friendly as it was ordered by top leaders. All rival gangs, want, contract terms immediately, requesting to be placed in, the FELON K-BOX ARENA. To work out their differences, in a controlled, civilized environment.

There is peace in all the prisons, and the list of fighters, increase rapidly. The violent convicts, show their true colors of human nature comes out. As they do not care, who, they kill. As for the list is now long. Many matches to choose from. Some want to fight, and just want to kill. As they did before in public, but got away with it.

This new form of discipline is overwhelmed, with volunteer fighters. As most, that joined, had to sign waivers, and admit they had killed before, or admit they will kill in public, in order to qualify for the matches. The true blood of these criminals truly just love, killing for fun, Being victorious would give them more rewards, and prizes inside the prison for winning the fights, rather then being out in society stealing, and killing for their greedy appetites.

There were over 30,990 of the prison inmate population that signed up, and admitted to unsolved murders. Admitted they wanted to kill, and nothing would stop their thirst for the rush, and satisfaction that killing would provide the inmates. If released. Since control fighting inside approved prison blocks is legal for felon life inmates, to fight. They are granted on equal agreement of fighting, to the death, with surviving benefits.

This sport took over so many ratings that most other sports that were televised had the players of the other sports watching the fights live, instead of playing, their sports. Viral was to slow, to describe. How quick it became a sensation of watching over any, ball throwing sports. The national sports broadcasters, had no choice but, played reruns while the fights were being broad casted.

The fights got so popular that terrorist groups wanted to battle in these fights to the death, and challenges to be put on the fights. 12 national treaties were signed, and any foreign participants were welcomed to participate. Soon many terrorist groups lined up to be allowed to fight to the death. AR1 prison blocks in Israel were made all around the world, and networked to Telenetvision, to the entire planet.

There was now peace on all the planet. There were no more wars, as the violent men with the uncontrollable rage to fight were still fighting. Their souls were marked the day they were born, and allowed to change. They instead chose their outcomes. To the 4 doors of the kill box. The terrorists that killed the life inmates

got lavished with many perks to themselves,
including the families of the fighters.

As all participating inmates were
permanent residents in the AR1 prison
blocks. To be criminals, were taken off the
streets. Countries around the world were
becoming slowly safer, from spontaneous
violent occurrences.

This would allow no other human to
be hurt in public places. Revenge, use to be
submitted in public places, innocent
children got hurt, and that was the last
straw for society to end the violence. War
in the veins of humanity has been since our
greatest grand kids of all. Cain. Those that
were direct from the seeds from
distributions have, and always be without

blemished, unless with Cain's blemished
blood.

The seed of Cain will terminate
himself as his DNA, has been programmed with
that vision for eternity. So it was
determined when God is ready to take the
life of a human, God will take the breath of
life from them, no matter what.

But those with the seeds of
violence, will erupt in war, and go out, and
kill. Wars have not stopped, or crimes to
society of thieving to become, take mans
plunders, with no remorse. There has to be
one world law, and one law only, for society
to change. This will not stop natural
disasters from taking lives of children, but
will control, the violent outburst, that
society has had since the beginnings.

Allowing the rage, and fights to
continue determined the fate of humans lives
to be taken from God, and the fate he had
for them. Either way if a man was going to
die out in public, or in a controlled room,
allowing passage to the next chapters God
has in store, for dead people. Innocent
victims, children especially, will be saved
in the billions, for the future.

Those petty thieves that shoot, and
kill, in robberies will be allowed to have a
life style better then most millionaires in
the Wardens, guarded mansion. Till the
inmate expires in a fight, or chooses not to
fight anymore, and lives his life, in his
cell. The inmate would be allowed to send
monies to their families, if they win, in
the fights.

The seed will slowly but surely be an extinction. The crime mobs, gangs, solo thieves, and anyone within the evil circle, in the outside world respected the rules. Society has become a new world order. Anyone, would be killed, with their families watching, for breaking the rules. With violence, or doing Haynes crimes. The crime rates all over the world become 99.7 percent contained the following years.

The ones, who do not follow the rule, were sent to prison. The people who volunteered to do voluntary manslaughter, were master fighters, and just wanted to kill. The majority were just violent criminals, that wanted the fortune winning the matches, and getting high off whatever substances they wanted. And yes the Wardens

Mansion did have many over dosing inmates.
The mansion had the best medical
professionals working there to save the
inmates if over dosing, as the Wardens
wanted them alive to perform in future
tournaments. Some inmates did die from over
dosing, but the majority lived, to fight
another day. Till the inmates finally
expired, in their last fights, of rage.

These rival gangs signed up to have
a fight against other rival gang to compete
against the gang, on an, all out fight
against each other, in the FELON K-BOX
ARENA. A controlled environment. The Warden
allowed these matches to happen after
everyone confessed to all the past crimes.
That would only be punishable by a death
sentence. The gang leaders, did not care
since the gang members they chose, were

already in prison for life. It was an easy
pick-en for the fights. The gang members in
this event all agreed to battle out to the
death. As it was their calling, and they
knew it was written.

Nobody's children, or grandparents,
will get hurt, from a stray bullet, that was
just in the wrong place in the wrong time.
From tragic events, of robberies of small
amounts of cash. And for what, a few lousy
worthless material items. It could never
replace a loved human victim, these
culprits, took, forever.

Room 4, is the allowance, of the
inmate, fighter, soldier, or Demon, to be
released in a controlled environment. With
money greater than the felons, would of made
in 2 life times. The rewards for these

thugs, bullies, felons, need to be released. The time bomb is ticking.

It will be 2666 soon. It will be 2022. It will be 1980. It will be 2222. It will be 1999. It will be 2001. It will be 2012. It will be 2033, until the human race unites? Unity could of happened any of those years. But humans, chose not to do anything about it.

The newspapers, and media, put the news that sells most. That is what is placed, on the front page. What tragedy will you read in that diverse year, of criminals that got away? Let them win in their minds, and be away from the hurtful victims.

No more, NO CAN DO!

CHAPTER THIRTEEN

The Gift

33 Crystal Skulls & The Anti+Christ
UNCENSORED, UNEDITED, RETRACTED INVENTION VERSION

1ST EDITION MANUSCRIPT. BOOK 5 OF 7

E-BOOK   978-1-967897-05-6
PAPERBACK   978-1-967897-15-5
HARDCOVER

**33 Crystal Skulls & The Anti+Christ
Chapter 11 & 12, PART 5 OF 7**

33 Crystal Skulls & The Anti+Christ

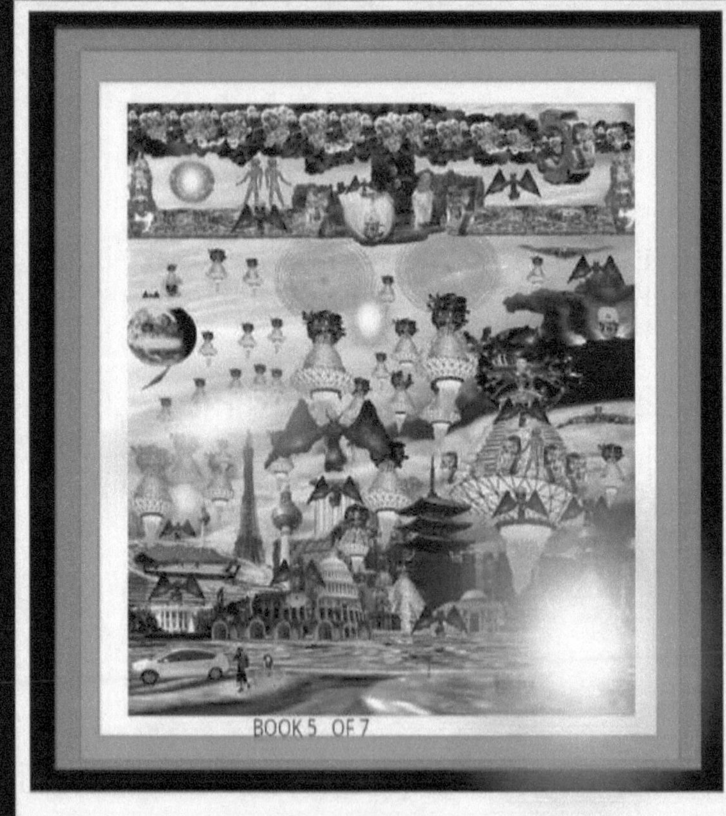